Globalisation and Sustainable Agriculture

A Christian Ethical Response

ii

Globalisation and Sustainable Agriculture

A Christian Ethical Response

Jobby John

2011

Globalisation and Sustainable Agriculture – Published by the Rev. Dr. Ashish Amos of Indian Society for Promoting Christian Knowledge (ISPCK), Post Box 1585, 1654 Madarsa Road, Kashmere Gate, Delhi-110006.

© Author, 2011

That the book in its original form titled "**A Christian Ethical Appraisal of the Impact of Globalization on Agriculture in India, with Special Reference to Vandana Shiva's Advocacy of Alternative Sustainable Agriculture**" is the thesis submitted to the Senate of Seampore College, towards the M.Th. degree and is published with written permission.

ISBN: 978-81-8465-188-1

Laser typeset by **ISPCK,** Post Box 1585,
1654 Madarsa Road, Kashmere Gate, Delhi-110006
Tel: 23866322, 23866323
e-mail–ashish@ispck.org.in • ella@ispck.org.in
website-www.ispck.org.

This book is dedicated to thousands of farmers, especially in Wayanad who had to sacrifice their lives due to the bashing infringement of the surplus mongers. Salute to Comrades who are tirelessly in the forefront to minimize the annihilation.

CONTENTS

Chapter 1

**Introduction and Different Approaches
to Agricultural Globalisation**

ABSTRACT

Globalisation which is conceived to be an irretrievable process has brought about significant changes in several aspects of life in India. The researcher, in particular, has tried to explore the impact of globalisation upon the predominantly agrarian economy of India. The researcher has also attempted to evaluate the impact of technological innovations on nature and its sustainability and a critical appraisal is done on monoculture-based and genetically-modified productivity, which are justified in terms of better production and rigorous economic growth. The major ethical contention is whether globalisation really ushers in the appropriate mode of agricultural production, which will help growth, development, and can maintain sustainability, while at the same time bring about just and equitable distribution.

In this research, the researcher has tried to evaluate the developments in agriculture sector, aided by Vandana Shiva's analysis, a third world academician-cum-activist who vociferously critiques the contemporary developments in the agricultural sector who proposes biodiversity-based production and traditional forms to be the model for a sustainable and healthy lifestyle leading to a better production system. The research is also aided by E.F. Schumacher's method of sustainable growth, protection and development paradigm. For Schumacher as well as Vandana Shiva, alternative models of agriculture are those that deal with life and its products, and are the results of processes of life and its means of production through the living soil.

The writer has dealt with the economy behind the globalisation of agriculture and its implications for future. Attempts to revitalise biodiversity-based productivity, its ecological significance, and its feasibility as a sustainable alternative model for development are asserted. In spite of being considering economic growth as one of the components of growth, treating agriculture as a mere economic category, which brings in profit is a derogatory attitude, hence the idea of treating agriculture as just another industry is contested. It is asserted that sustainability is primary and not trade, in order to cater as well to the future generations.

ACKNOWLEDGEMENTS

My earnest thanks to all those who have supplemented my spiritual journey so far. I am overwhelmingly honoured by the foreword and preface written by Dr. Vandana Shiva and Rev. Dr. K.C. Abraham for my first effort. I am indebted to both these internationally reputed scholars of which Dr. K.C. Abraham stands as a seed sower who has inspired me to think in terms of issues relating to the vulnerable masses of our nation. Dr. Vandana Shiva's writings and ecological activism has inspired me to explore more into the avenues of my study. My sincere thanks to Dr. John Mohan Razu who has challenged me during my theological training at United Theological College, Bangalore. My love and thanks to the UTC community that made me struggle, analyse, explore and critically evaluate the nuances of social and Biblical experiences.

I cannot forget my loving parents, Kulathumkal Philipose John and Molly John who are persons of great faith and simple life. My family comprising my wife– Halish, my daughters—Athira and Ann have been supportive all through to give me a pleasant atmosphere.

Special thanks to Ms. Whyneeta William for designing the cover and Deepak Masih for type setting.

FOREWORD

"Globalisation has reduced life to economy, and the economy has been further reduced to a corporate economy. This is an ethical issue, because it decides who controls food and agriculture, it determines the fate of diverse species, it determines whether small farmers live or die, or whether children are allowed to live. Each of these issues is a deep ethical issue. As a result of globalisation, five giant agribusiness corporations control trade in food and five giant biotechnology corporations control the seed. Monsanto controls 95% of the cotton seed supply in India with its Bt. cotton. As a result of high costs, farmers are in debt, and indebted farmers are committing suicide. 250,000 Indian farmers have committed suicide since globalisation of agriculture started. Every 4th Indian is now hungry, and every second child is "wasted" because of severe malnutrition.

These tragedies are a consequence of a very narrow understanding of economy which leaves out nature and people, and only focuses on corporate profit and calls it growth.

We need to view food and agriculture in its ethical and ecological context.

I am happy that Rev. Jobby John has taken up this challenge in his thesis.

We need many more Rev. John's so that the ethical fabric of our society can be strengthened and again, and poor may have justice."

- Dr. Vandana Shiva

PREFACE

I am happy that the thesis presented for his M.Th degree by the Rev. Jobby John is now made available for the wider public. Jobby John is an able student in Christian ethics, a discipline of study that integrates Christian insights with an analysis of contemporary socio-political and economic realities. It is most impressive that he ventured to do research, not in a text-book topic but in a challenging and complex reality that affects the lives of ordinary people, the poor and middle-level farmers in our country.

The impact of globalisation is all pervasive. Not a single sector of our society is unaffected by it. The farming community in India, quite contrary to the claims of planners and wielders of power is being sucked into the global system that is detrimental to their interests. Jobby John has carefully analysed this process from the perspective of the farmers who are the losers by globalisation. The development paradigm that is uncritically adopted by the dominant actors is critically looked at in this book. Borrowing the insights from the great ecological activist, Vandana Shiva and the economist Shumacher, the author argues for a new paradigm that is farmer friendly and by *ipso facto* earth friendly. Sustainable growth, Bio-Diversity that presupposes a shift from "trade first" to "food first" and "corporation first" to "farmer first" — are the concepts proposed in this thesis.

The book concludes with a brief biblical/theological reflection that could be enlarged. I sincerely hope that this study will generate further discussions and provide a inspiration to scholars for undertaking similar research that is relevant and helpful to the cause of the marginalised.

Dr. K.C. Abraham
Former Direcgor of SATHRI,
A Research Programme of the
Senate of Serampore College and
Professor of Theology and Ethics at
United Theological College, Bangalore.

INTRODUCTION

Globalisation has brought about significant changes in many aspects of life in India. Changes are happening in most sectors of which the agriculture sector is no exception. Indian economy is predominantly an agrarian economy and most of the labour force is involved in agriculture and related activities. Since the 1990's the agriculture sector has undergone drastic transformation and significant changes have come about in the relations of production and social relations, for which many claim that globalisation is responsible. Biotechnological innovations have brought in monoculture-based and genetically- modified productivity, which are justified in terms of better production, and rigorous economic growth. For some, these changes are positive, nevertheless the major ethical contention is whether globalisation really ushers in the appropriate mode of agricultural production, which will help growth, development, and can maintain sustainability, while at the same time bring about just and equitable distribution.

Vandana Shiva, as a third world academician-cum-activist, vociferously critiques the contemporary developments in the agricultural sector. She proposes biodiversity-based production and traditional forms to be the model for a sustainable and healthy lifestyle leading to a better production system. The writer would like to deal with the economy behind the globalisation of agriculture, whether this will benefit the Indian masses or hamper the whole agriculture sector. It is in this light that attempts made by Vandana Shiva to revitalise biodiversity-based productivity, its influence, impact, and its feasibility as a sustainable alternative model for development will be evaluated.

Method of Study

Apart from the available library materials, the writer will be analysing the agriculture sector from the point of view of E.F. Schumacher's method of sustainable growth, protection and development. For Schumacher as well as Vandana Shiva, alternative models of agriculture are those that deal with life and its products, and are the results of processes of life and its means of production through the living soil. However the fundamental principle of modernity is that it deals with human-devised processes which work reliably only when applied to human-devised, non-living materials. Treating agriculture as an economic category, which brings in profit is a derogatory attitude, hence they contest the idea of treating agriculture as just another industry. Along with this, Vandana Shiva's proposals for a sustainable agriculture and critical appraisal of her patent laws and protectionism will also be examined.

ABBREVIATIONS

AoA	Agreement on Agriculture
EU	European Union
FAO	Food and Agriculture Organisation
GATT	General Agreement on Trade and Tariff
GDP	Gross Domestic Product
IDB	Industrial Development Bank
IMF	International Monetary Fund
MNC	Multi National Company
NAAS	National Academy of Agricultural Sciences
NEP	New Economic Policies
NGO	Non-Governmental Organisations
QR	Quantitative Restrictions
SAP	Structural Adjustment Policies
TNC	Trans National Companies
TRIPS	Trade Related Intellectual Property Rights
UNDP	United Nations Development Programme
U.S	United States
WB	World Bank
WDR	World Development Report
WSF	World Social Forum
W.T.O	World Trade Organisation

Chapter 1

INTRODUCTION AND DIFFERENT APPROACHES TO AGRICULTURAL GLOBALISATION

1. Introduction

Globalisation in general and Globalisation of agriculture is a reality that is captivating all around the globe albeit tough resistances. The proponents of the process of globalisation argue that market related competition and exchanges will enhance the less-developed nations to compete with developed nations. Further more, for them; the trickle-down effect will also benefit the under-developed nations. While the opportunities and benefits of this process have been stressed by its proponents and supporters, recently there has been increasing disillusionment among many policy-makers in the South, analysts and academics, as well as the community of non-governmental organisations (NGO's) in both South and the North. The reasons for resisting the process are multi-faceted. Among the important factors are the lack of tangible benefits to most developing countries from opening their economies, despite the well-publicised claims of export and income gains; the economic losses and social dislocation that are being caused to many developing countries by rapid financial and trade liberalisation; the growing inequalities of wealth and opportunities arising from globalisation; and the perception that environmental, social and cultural problems have been made worse by workings of the global free- market economy[1]. 'Globalisation' according to the opponents is a very uneven process, with unequal distribution of benefits and losses. This imbalance leads to polarisation between the few countries and groups that gain, and the many countries and groups in society that lose out or are marginalised. Furthermore, opponents argue that the unethical means through which competition is initiated in the global market will benefit only a section of the market monopolies and will further disintegrate a sustainable agriculture growth.

2. What is Agricultural Globalisation?

Toeing the globalisation process, agriculture sector is no exception from integrating into the world order of competition. In order to enable competition, integration of economies through trade liberalisation policies is envisaged. Trade liberalisation is supposed to bring benefits to national agricultural economies. The idea is that local farmer must not be confined only to the domestic market but must have access to the global market. The new ideology is centered around export strategies and gives lesser attention to food security. Thus the proponents claim that there is a focal shift in the sector. For them, there are strong reasons to suppose that trade liberalisation will benefit the poor, the people of the less-developed nations. Previously, the 'food security' concept has prevented the farmers from exporting agricultural commodities, particularly cereals such as wheat, and rice on the ground that it would lead to scarcity at home. Earlier there was an idea that we could export only if there was a surplus,

---

[1] Martin Khor, *Rethinking Globalization* (Bangalore: Books for Change, 2001), 1.

and import in case of deficit[2]. But there has been a change in thinking. It actually means that exports and imports would depend on international and domestic prices and not on physical availability and comparative advantage[3]. Another assumption is that, in tune with the growing population worldwide and in order to feed the millions of poor around the world, agricultural productivity need to be intensified. Intensify agricultural production and manage land and water to feed a growing and increasingly urban population[4].

3. Converging Ideas in Favour of Agricultural Globalisation

a. Globalising Agriculture: The Proposed Projects

Opening up the economies is one of the primary essentials that boost growth according to the proponents of agricultural globalisation. In so far as the evidence gives us a lead, it suggests that openness is a particularly important component of reform[5]. Openness seems to promote growth in the poorest countries at least as well as in others[6]. The path prescribed for poor countries in the 2003 United Nations Development Programme (UNDP) study is export expansion[7]. The government has embarked on a policy which will gradually free agro exports from

---

[2] Brojendra Nath Banerjee, "Globalization of Agriculture", *Religion And Society*, Vol. XLI, No. 2, (June 1994), 53.

[3] *Ibid.*

[4] World Development Report 2003, *Sustainable Development in a Dynamic World Transforming Institutions, Growth and Quality of Life* (New York: Oxford University Press, 2003), 83

[5] Andrew Berg, Anne Krueger, "Lifting All Boats", *Finance and Development* (September, 2002), 18.

[6] *Ibid.*, 18.

[7] Emma Bonino, Benedetto Della Vedova, "Make WTO Work, Alternative is Worse", *Deccan Herald*, (Tuesday, September 2, 2003).

the shackles of controls, allowing the farmer a choice between domestic sales and exports; at the same time it will ensure that the domestic consumer is not starved by supply, which if need be, will be supplemented from abroad[8]. The new-found policy seeks to insulate agro-exports from the vagaries of domestic market conditions and exports need no longer be a residues derived from domestic surplus[9]. Under the increasing outward-looking policy, the decision to export would be determined to a large extent by the advantages in the global market[10].

b. Enabling Competitiveness: A Development Paradigm

Globalisation is not free of an ideological thrust. The development process is about change and transformation. For the proponents, the ideology is that of development, a paradigm inclusive of free trade and liberalisation policies that which enable growth. Poor countries could boost growth and reduce poverty by expanding exports to the rich countries and to each other[11]. In his inaugural address, R. S. Paroda (Indian Council of Agricultural Research*A report on the national workshop of' Globalisation of Agriculture: Research and Development in India', organised by the National Academy of Agricultural Sciences (NAAS) at the Kerala Agricultural University Main Campus, Trichur, during 2–3 February 2001) said that globalisation is now an irreversible process and is not a mere economic and financial phenomenon[12]. Liberalisation of agricultural trade has resulted in

---

[8] Brojendra...54.

[9] *Ibid.*

[10] Brojendra...54.

[11] Hans Peter Lankes, "Market Access For Developing Countries", *Finance and Development* (September, 2002), 8.

[12] From the archives, Current Science, Vol. 80, NO. 12, 25 June 2001. 1481.

increased globalisation of Indian agriculture. The share of agricultural trade in agricultural GDP has increased from about 6 per cent per annum during the triennium ending 1990–1991 (before liberalisation) to about 9 per cent in the late 1990s[13].

c. Genetic Engineering and High Yielding: A Vision Enabling Future

The development of industry based production system that is heavily dependent upon the scientific and technological advancement is expected to stimulate the scientific and technological advancement in the third world through open trade policies. The other side of globalisation is technology, which has defined the character of globalisation in a large measure and its own character being influenced by it[14]. Agricultural growth is envisioned to escalate through the one-dimensional monoculture paradigm of increasing agricultural productivity and genetic engineering constitutes to this strategy. Genetic engineering is the method of changing the inherited characteristics of an organism in a predetermined way by altering its genetic material and this is often done to cause micro-organisms, such as bacteria or viruses, to synthesise increased yields of compounds, to form entirely new compounds, or to adapt to different environments[15]. However, there are divergent views on the role of genetic engineering/ biotechnology in bringing about sustainable development. The mainstream view is that this will feed the world, cure diseases once thought to be incurable,

---

[13] *Ibid.*, 1481.

[14] Ambirajan. S, *"Globalization, Technology, Media & Culture"*, Paper prepared for discussion at the UTC, (Bangalore, 29th July-1998), 5.

[15] "Genetic Engineering", *Microsoft® Encarta® 99 Encyclopedia*. © 1993-1998 Microsoft Corporation.

clean up the environment, and even increase biodiversity[16]. It is an inevitable development of science and technology and it makes no sense to fight against it. On the other hand, there are many who contest these promises and claims. They also question the soundness and ethics of the science which underpins genetic engineering. Indigenous peoples belong to this later category.

d. Global Institutions Behind the Paradigm

Global institutions play an important role in a rapidly globalising world. Global institutions, which are capable of investing large capitals, are supposed to be the backbone of this developing process. The agreement on Agriculture of the W.T.O builds on the Trade liberalisation policies of the World Bank and the IMF[17]. The developing countries had been drawn into the process of financial liberalisation due partly to advice given by international financial institutions, and to mainstream view that there were great benefits to be derived from opening up to inflows of international capital[18]. The World Trade Organisation (WTO) appears committed to removing all "barriers" to international trade, to achieve "free trade," and thus, to removing all "economic boundaries" among nations[19].

e. Structural Adjustment Programme

An important component of structural adjustment programmes is the rationalisation or streamlining of public

---

[16] Victoria Tauli- Corpuz, "Biotechnology and Indigenous People Source", *www.thirdworldnetwork.org.*

[17] Vandana Shiva, Afsar H.Jafri and Kunwar Jalees, eds., How Globalization is Destroying Farmers and Livelihoods (New Delhi: Navdanya Research Foundation for Science, Technology and Ecology), 11.

[18] Martin Khor, *Rethinking Globalization* (Bangalore: Books for Change, 2001), 55.

[19] John E. Ikerd, *http://www.ssu.missouri.edu/Faculty/JIkerd/papers/ TorontoGlobalization.html*

sector enterprises. The assumption is that production in the public sector is inherently more inefficient that in the private sector. Another demand of SAP is the elimination of food subsidies, agricultural subsidies etc. accompanied by a systematic pairing down of the system of public distribution of food. Developing nations are urged to reduce domestic subsidies to farmers and remove non-tariff controls on agricultural products, converting these to tariffs and then progressively reducing these tariffs[20].

f. W.T.O and Agricultural Globalisation

The Agreement on Agriculture of the W.T.O. builds on the Trade liberalisation policies of the World Bank and IMF. The Agreement on Agriculture has three sections[21]:

1) Export competition or export liberalisation (Article 9).

2) Market access or import liberalisation (Article 4).

3) Domestic support or reduction of domestic subsidies (Article 6).

g. External Liberalisation and Internal Liberalisation

The free trade zones are supposed to be the decisive factor in the process of globalisation. The inter relatedness of world nations are supposed to widen through the trade liberalisation policies. Liberalisation policies are aimed at relaxing both external as well as internal[22] policies. The external liberalisation of national economies involves

---

[20] Martin Khor, ...*Rethinking Globalization* 44.

[21] Vandana Shiva, Afsar.H.Jafri and Kunwar Jalees, eds., *The Mirage of Market Access* (New Delhi: Navadanya Research Foundation for Science, Technology and Ecology, 2003), 12.

[22] Nation states are forced to relax national policies on food security, subsidies etc. according to the guidelines set up by international organizations such as World Bank and the IMF.

breaking down national barriers to economic activities, resulting in greater openness and integration of countries in the world markets[23]. The proponents claim that these liberalisation policies have shown significant changes in course of time. Trade has been an engine of growth for the past 50 years, owing in part to eight successive rounds of multilateral trade liberalisation[24]. Over the past 20 years, world trade has grown twice as fast as world real GDP (6 percent versus 3percent), deepening economic integration and raising living standards[25]. Also, trade liberalisation tends to reduce monopoly rents and the value of connections to bureaucratic and political power[26]. In developing countries it may be expected to increase the relative wage of low-skilled workers, who are likely to be scarcer in the more developed world economy than at home. Liberalisation of agriculture may increase rural incomes[27].

4. Approaches as Against Agricultural Globalisation

a. *Trade Liberalisation Promoting Growth- A Fallacy*

Globalisation claims and promises that its processes would usher in development and growth. The benefits and costs of trade liberalisation especially in the agriculture sector for developing countries constitute an increasingly controversial issue. The conventional view that trade liberalisation is necessary and has automatic and generally positive effects for development is being challenged

---

[23] Martin Khor, ...*Rethinking Globalization*, 8.

[24] Anne McGuirk, "The Doha Development Agenda", *Finance and Development* (September, 2002), 4.

[25] *Ibid.*, 4.

[26] Andrew Berg and Anne Krueger, "Lifting All Boats", *Finance and Development* (September, 2002), 18.

[27] *Ibid.*, 18.

empirically and analytically[28]. *The Agriculture Agreement was supposed to result in import liberalisation and reduction of domestic support and export subsidies for agricultural products, especially in the rich countries, and this was expected to improve the market access of those Southern countries that export agricultural products. As it turned out, however, the protection and subsidies have been allowed to remain very high. For example, in the initial year of agreement, there were very high tariffs in the United States (sugar 244 per cent, peanuts 174 per cent); the EU (beef 213 per cent, wheat 168 per cent); Japan (wheat 353 percent), and Canada (butter 360 per cent, eggs 236 per cent) (Das, 1998:59). The rich countries have had to reduce such high rates by only 36 per cent on average to the end of 2000. The tariffs have thus still been very high, making it impossible for developing countries' exports to gain access. Also, the agreement has allowed the developed countries to maintain most of the high subsidies that existed prior to the Uruguay Round conclusion. For example, they are obliged to reduce their very high domestic subsidies by only 20 per cent. In contrast, most developing countries had little or no domestic or export subsidies earlier. They are now barred by the Agriculture Agreement from having then or raising them in future (Das, 1998:62)*[29]. Many developing countries notice and are actively complaining that trade liberalisation has produced negative results for their economies or has marginalised them. The world trading system has been favoring the exporters of manufactured goods, while proving to be disadvantageous to the many developing countries whose main participation in global trade has consisted in the export of raw materials and commodities and the import of finished products[30].

---

[28] Martin Khor,... *Rethinking Globalization*, 32.

[29] *Ibid.*, 41.

[30] *Op.cit.*, 29.

b. Global Competitiveness: A Myth

For those who oppose globalisation of Agriculture, 'Global Competitiveness' initiated through globalisation didn't initiate developing nations into the 'competing fold'. The path prescribed for poor countries in the 2003 United Nations Programme study is export expansion. But this has been extremely difficult since rich countries are doing little to make their markets more accessible to poor countries' products, neither reducing tariffs and subsidies nor eliminating quotas. A recent Food and Agriculture Organisation (FAO) study of the experience of 16 developing countries in implementing the Uruguay Round Agriculture Agreement concluded that: 'A common reported concern was with a general trend towards the concentration of farms. In the virtual absence of safety nets, the process also marginalised small producers and added to unemployment and poverty. Similarly, most studies pointed to continued problems of adjustment'[31]. On the contrary, it is argued that developed nations are misusing the agreements and thereby are the beneficiaries. In 1991, when the Dunkel Draft Text of the GATT Agreement was finalised, we had predicted that given the high subsidies to rich farmers in rich countries, and given the power of global corporations, trade liberalisation of agriculture would be a death knell for Indian farmers and eight years after the coming into force of the WTO, poor peasants are being annihilated by the policies and the rules of globalisation[32]. Moreover the Structural Adjustment measures introduced as part of the World Bank-IMF strategies for countries like India has pushed

---

[31] *Ibid.*, 44.

[32] Vandana Shiva, Afsar.H.Jafri and Kunwar Jalees, eds.,... *The Mirage of Market Access*, 5.

the country deep into debt. As a result of Structural Adjustment measures introduced in 1991, the total debt of India had increased from ₹ 280,746 crore in 1992-93 to ₹ 429,271 crore in 2000 (provisional) and the debt service has increased from US $ 507 million to US $ 8645 million in 1994, which is neatly a 20-fold increase[33]. The Human Development Report 1996 showed that over the past three decades, only 15 countries have enjoyed high growth, while 89 countries were worse off economically that they were 10 or more years earlier[34]. 'Economic' gains have benefited greatly a few countries, at the expense of many', said the report.

> The continuously unfolding scenario also underlines the need for re-examining the purpose and working mechanism of the WTO. It is becoming all the more clear that the WTO, instead of helping free trade is actually hindering it and unbalanced negotiations between the powerful and the weak are a facile weapon in the hands of the developed countries. It is a myth that free trade and trade negotiations are possible under the WTO[35].

c. Monoculture Destabilises Sustainability

The introduction of uniformity is justified as a trade-off for raising yields of horticultural crops miraculously[36]. However it is contested that monoculture destabilises sustainability and increases food insecurity for various reasons.

---

[33] Vandana Shiva, Afsar.H.Jafri and Kunwar Jalees, eds., *The Mirage of Market Access* (New Delhi: Navadanya Research Foundation for Science, Technology and Ecology, 2003), 16.

[34] Martin Khor,... *Rethinking Globalization.* 17.

[35] Editorial column: *People's Reporter*, Vol.19 Issue.13, Mumbai July 10-25, 2006.

[36] Vandana Shiva, Afsar.H.Jafri and Kunwar Jalees, eds., *The Mirage of Market Access*, 63.

The impact of the new agriculture policy has been to promote a shift from food grains to vegetable sand perishable commodities. While grains can be stored and consumed locally, potatoes and tomatoes must be sold immediately. A vegetable centered policy thus decreases food security and increases farmers' vulnerability to the market. While this promotes monocultures of perishable commodities, the word used for these monocultures is "diversification" in typical globalisation doublespeak[37].

Because the Agriculture Agreement of W.T.O. is an agribusiness treaty it distorts production and trade from the perspective of nature, small farmers and all consumers, especially the poor[38].

d. Productivity Vs Food Insecurity

According to the free market ideology, the best way to fight hunger and improve the economic situation of farmers in developing countries is through trade and investment liberalisation, production for export, and cuts in domestic support. Increasing agricultural production is envisioned to be the best cure to combat poverty in agricultural- based developing nations. These policy changes, however, have severely undermined food security and the livelihood of small farmers in developing countries[39]. Globalisation has forced countries to give up food first policies and adopt export first policies. However, export first policies under trade liberalisation are destroying domestic food security and export earnings[40]. WTO's Agreement on Agriculture (AOA) paradigm favors

---

[37] Ibid., 62.

[38] Ibid., 7.

[39] Anuradha Mittal, *Land Loss, Poverty and Hunger* (International Forum on Globalization, December 3, 2001) *www.alternet.org*

[40] Vandana Shiva, Afsar.H.Jafri and Kunwar Jalees, eds., *The Mirage of Market Access* (New Delhi: Navadanya Research Foundation for Science, Technology and Ecology, 2003), 48.

capital-intensive and corporate agribusiness-driven agriculture, and is insensitive to the needs of the masses of peasantry and threatens the livelihood of the vast masses of the small and marginal farmers in developing countries such as India. Increased productivity is substituted with food security to ensure the growth of poor agriculturists in the developing nations. But this has brought about the local farmers in a vicious circle where in increasingly the private ownership and import liberalisation policies are threatening the local food subsistent economies.

e. Genetic Engineering: Unsustainability Sponsored

Genetic engineering methods are supposed to increase yields, but the opponents argue that this will lead to unsustainability. Genetic Engineering is the method of changing the inherited characteristics of an organism in a predetermined way by altering its genetic material. This is often done to cause micro-organisms, such as bacteria or viruses, to synthesise increased yields of compounds, to form entirely new compounds, or to adapt to different environments[41]. Spokespersons for U.S. agribusiness corporations such as Cargill, which already has large investments in the agribusiness, are busy urging countries to accept the 'logic' of relying more heavily on imported grains, so that its own farmers can devote themselves to specialty crops. The claim of the genetic engineering industry to precision, predictability and safety is not backed by its own experiences or by the science of genetics[42]. Examples are cited from different parts of the world to substantiate this. Exactly a year ago, the Genetic Engineering Approval Committee (GEAC) of the Union

---

[41] "Genetic Engineering", *Microsoft® Encarta® 99 Encyclopedia.* © 1993-1998 Microsoft Corporation

[42] Debashis Banerji, *What Ails Bt Cotton?* (The Hindu, 18.03.2003).

Ministry of Environment approved Bt. cotton for cultivation in India. Monsanto, the U.S agrochemical giant which provided the seeds, claims that more than 50,000 farmers planted Bt cotton in over 40,000 hectares[43]. The experience of these farmers has however been extremely uneven, with reports of crop failure and disappointments from all over India. According to R. Akhileshwari, promoting genetically engineered crops as a solution to world hunger is simply a means for corporates to control the world's food supply for profits. Experience in different parts of the world has shown that the genetically engineered seeds have sprouted disaster and misery for hundreds and thousands of farmers[44]. Those who oppose genetically engineered methods as substitute to the traditional farming methods argue that genetic engineering leads to unsustainability. The two-day public forum on genetic engineering, agriculture and farmers rights held in Hyderabad emphasised that it is the farmers and farming communities in the Indian subcontinent that are keeping diversity alive and categorically stated that there is no place for transgenic crops in Asia or elsewhere in the world[45].

f. Economic Agenda: A Capitalist Agenda

Globalisation, for the opponents, is not free of ideology, rather is toeing a Capitalist ideology. Lenin argues that an international system of exploitation develops out of the social relations of capitalist production. According to him the earliest phase of capitalism is highly competitive as emerging capitalists seek to maximise profit at the expense of others. However as some become more

---

[43] *Ibid.*

[44] R.Akhileshwari, *A New Colonisation* (Sunday Spotlight, ...).

[45] *Ibid.*

successful, and as the rate of profit falls, unevenness between firms in the capitalist market leads to the monopolisation of its sectors as companies are forced out or absorbed by their more successful competitors[46].

> I argue that globalisation is much a structural reality as a social construction- an imagined economic order of the future that involves both a value judgment and an ideological stand. Globalisation is a structural change. The increasing flow of capital, goods and technology, and the demands for bigger mutual market access have instead driven the whole world into an era in which resources have to be allocated more efficiently...the ideological bubble regarding globalisation reflects not only the conflicts of material interests but also the tensions between globalisation and the established norms and values of each country[47].

"Globalisation is borderless invasion by the super power and it creates political instability in the midst of religious complexity in Asia. The new forces that make the new world order are economic and market driven and they lead to the establishment of a new empire. The God that Bush worships is not our God"[48].

g. Third World Agricultural Economies in Tantrum

For those who oppose agricultural globalisation, the Agriculture Agreement could have severe negative effects on many Third World countries. Most of them will have to reduce domestic subsidies of farmers and remove non-tariff controls on agricultural products, converting these

---

[46] Malcom Waters, *Globalization* (London: Routledge, 1995), 2.

[47] Quoted by I.John Mohan Razu, *Ideology of Life and Theology of Resistance: A Framework for the Present* (Bangalore: BTF, 2001), 143.

[48] Pradit Takerngrangsarit, "The God that Bush Worships is not Our God", *People's Reporter* (Mumbai Vol.19, Issue 20, October 25- November 10, 2006), 1.

to tariffs and then progressively reducing these tariffs. Analytical studies substantiate these arguments. On a rough estimate, Indian peasants are loosing more than ₹ 1162 billion ($26 billion US dollars) per year due to falling farm prices in every commodity, staple foods and cash crops[49]. Whether it is export liberalisation or export liberalisation Third world farmers are getting hurt. 'Market access' has turned out to be a mirage. India's food production has declined by 12% in one year[50]. Five million peasants' livelihoods have disappeared in India since "reforms" were introduced[51]. Many Southern countries have lost their self-reliance in terms of producing their own food, as lands were converted to farm export crops that in many cases yielded unsatisfactory results in terms of instability of price and demand[52].

h. Destabilising the Agricultural Economies: A Conspiracy

Opening Southern markets and converting peasant agriculture to corporate agriculture is the primary aim of Cargill and hence the Agreement on Agriculture[53]. For Cargill, capturing Asian markets is key. Asia happens to be the largest agriculture economy of the world, with the majority involved in agriculture. Converting self-sufficient food economies in to food dependent economies is the Cargill vision and the W.T.O strategy[54]. America is now

---

[49] Vandana Shiva, Afsar.H.Jafri and Kunwar Jalees, eds.,... *The Mirage of Market Access*, 5.

[50] *Ibid.*, 5.

[51] *Ibid.*, 8.

[52] Martin Khor,... *Rethinking Globalization*, 29.

[53] The Agreement on Agriculture should be called a Cargill Agreement. It was former Cargill Vice-President, Dan Amstutz who drafted the original text of the Uruguay Round Agreement on Agriculture.

[54] Vandana Shiva, Afsar.H.Jafri and Kunwar Jalees, eds., ...7.

targeting its food and agriculture toward the 600 million 'new consumers' in Asia and Southeast Asia and another 400 million in Latin America and Central America; in other words, America intends to meet the food security needs of the estimated 1 billion 'new consumers' in South and Southeast Asia and in Latin and Central America thereby depriving and displacing the local producers and farmers from their only means of livelihood[55]. Once these countries become dependent on the U.S. and other developed countries for food, the basic human rights, the battle for food supremacy is won.

In spite of the two vital standpoints; one being uncritically supporting agricultural globalisation and the other offering vehement critique; there is yet another group which consider selective globalisation or a controlled from of globalisation. For them, globalisation ushers certain benefits under the supervision of state-sponsored development programme. According to them, the government has to play an important role in stimulating and sustaining economic activities. Economic reforms should be made more gradually, and be more meaningful. Liberalisation and deregulation for them is a short term therapy. This position reiterates that in the agriculture sector, an attempt should be made to balance the demand of efficiency or productivity with the requirement of equity and justice. According to Brojendra Nath Banerjee[56], India has opportunities to benefit from globalising agriculture. For him, some restrictions have to be maintained while ensuring that agriculture sector should not be thrown into the absolute hands for the market forces. Furthermore,

---

[55] *www.fpif.org/outside/commentary/2002/0202food_body.html.*

[56] Dr. Brojendra Nath Banerjee, is a well-known author of books on Economic Development and International relations, Environment and Religion.

quick liberalisation should not be the agenda in the agriculture sector. For Brojendra Nath Banerjee, the experience of the East Asian economies reflect that there can be large income generation through reform in the agriculture sector, even while imperfections exist within the system.

Chapter 2

GLOBALISATION OF AGRICULTURE AND ITS IMPACT IN INDIA

1. Introduction

In the first chapter, attempts are made to trace out the different views emerged in relation to agricultural globalisation. An attempt is taken in this chapter to evaluate the emergent policies, its economic and social implications in the predominantly agricultural Indian economy. Whether encouraging or disruptive, it is a subject of fact that globalisation and its processes exert its own impact on the agriculture sector worldwide. It is also apparent that the effects are visible in the policy making bodies of both the 'developed' and the 'third world' nations as well as the social milieu of the third world nations.

2. Economic Implications

a. Liberalisation Policies and the International Pressure on the Third World Nations like India

Liberalisation policies also known as New Economic Policies (NEP) is part and parcel of the globalising process.

> The New Economic Policy, in general, has the following components: 1) Liberalisation: abolishing industrial licensing system except for hazardous and environmentally sensitive industries; removing permission system for investment and expansion by monopoly houses; increasing the number of industries for private capital participation; and liberal access to foreign technology. 2) Privatisation: disinvestment in public sector undertakings with a view to broaden ownership and commercialising management. 3) Globalisation: integration of the national

economy in to the world economy by reducing controls and restrictions on imports, exports and inflow of foreign capital, and by allowing the exchange rate of rupee to be determined under competitive market conditions. 4) Fiscal reform: reduction in fiscal deficit, i.e. excesses of public expenditure over and above the government revenue receipts, by cutting government expenditure[1].

Apart from these, there are numerous international policies formulated like the GATT[2] treaty, in order to enhance the liberalising process. Once a country agrees to be part of the GATT treaty, and becomes part of it, it has to follow the guidelines of the IMF[3] and the World Bank. Liberalisation policies are guided largely by the policies formulated by international institutions like the IMF and the World Bank. These two financial institutions; IMF and World Bank, lend money to the developing nations with specific conditions. These financial institutions will decide guidelines related to economic reforms for each country and if not allowed, further assistance will not be considered. These sanctions will be reconsidered only at a stage when the respective countries achieve targets proposed by the IMF and the WB. This can be achieved only through liberalisation policies. All these exert pressure on the third world to toe the guidelines set by these international institutions. Noted trade union leader M.K.Pandhe has stated that "Globalisation has not come

---

[1] Abdul Aziz, "Manifestation of Globalization", in *Globalization-Marginalization of Women, Dalits and Tribals,* Viswanath Rosemanry, ed., (Bangalore: Solidarity, 1998), 12.

[2] General Agreement on Trade and Tariff; Agriculture has never been part of GATT. It was introduced during the Uruguay Round. The Agreement on Agriculture has three sections: 1) Export competition or export liberalization (Article 9). 2) Market access or import liberalization (Article 4). 3) Domestic support or reduction of domestic subsidies (Article 6).

[3] International Monetary Fund.

to stay but is being forced on us due to the dictates of the World Bank and developed countries. It is high time that we pressurise the government to withdraw the policies before the nation's economy is ruined"[4].

Liberalisation policies in the agriculture sector too toe similar policies. The agreement on Agriculture of the W.T.O. builds on the Trade Liberalisation policies of the World Bank and the IMF. There are five major sources of external liberalisation of agriculture in India[5]. 1) The Structural Adjustment Programmes (SAP) of the World Bank.2) The Agreement on Agriculture of the World Trade Organisation (WTO). 3) Bilateral Trade pressure from countries such as the U.S. 4) Internal policy pressure by TNC's in agribusiness.5) The commitment of experts and policy makers to the external liberalisation paradigm. According to Vandana Shiva, "External liberalisation is foreign trade and foreign investment driven liberalisation". External liberalisation, for her, serves the external interests. Agricultural liberalisation under SAP's[6] is an example of such external liberalisation. According to Vandana Shiva, it consists of the following elements[7]:

- Liberalising fertiliser imports and deregulating domestic manufacturing and the distribution of fertilisers

- Removing land ceiling regulation

---

[4] *Deccan Herald:* News Service, 27.04.2001, 5.

[5] Vandana Shiva, Afsar.H.Jafri and Kunwar Jalees, eds., *The Mirage of Market Access* (New Delhi: Navadanya Research Foundation for Science, Technology and Ecology, 2003), 11.

[6] Structural Adjustment Policies.

[7] Vandana Shiva, Afsar.H.Jafri and Kunwar Jalees, eds., *The Mirage of Market Access* (New Delhi: Navadanya Research Foundation for Science, Technology and Ecology, 2003), 11.

- Removing subsidies on irrigation, electricity and credit and creating conditions to facilitate the trading of canal irrigation water rights

- Deregulating the wheat, rice, sugarcane, cotton and edible oil and oilseed industries

- Dismantling food security system

- Removing controls on markets, traders and processors, and subsidies to cooperatives

- Abolishing the Essential Commodities Act, the general ban on futures trading, inventory control, selective credit controls on inventory financing

- Treating farmers' cooperatives on an equal footing with the private sector.

Liberalisation policies leading to such a 'regulated' situation under the supervision of international bodies like the IMF and the World Bank pressurise third world nations to regulate agricultural subsidies. In the liberalisation phase many of the controls and restrictions have been lifted. While discussion on the adverse impact of neo-liberal policy on the farm sector was going on in a number of workshops and seminars at the WSF[8] 2007 held at Nairobi, hundreds of farmers from Dominican republic, Africa, the Caribbean and the Pacific staged massive demonstrations protesting against the alarming threat to their livelihood when the markets are opened for tariff-free imports of agricultural goods from the US and Europe[9]. Due to withdrawal of several subsidies available to farmers under New Economic

---

[8] The World Social Forum (WSF) was started as a counterforce to the World Economic Forum (WEF) being held at Davos every year. The Nairobi event coincided with the WEF at Davos which was held this year, from 24 to 28 January.

[9] People's Reporter, "Protect the Farmers and Cancel the Debts" (Mumbai: Vol, 20, Issue 3, February 10-25, 2007), 1.

Policies dictated by the W.T.O., farmers are facing difficult situation in most states of India.

b. Subsidies, IMF-WB and W.T.O. Policies and Regulations

It is generally contended that the policies formulated by international financial institutions like the IMF and the World Bank are supportive to the developed nations rather than providing assistance to the third world nations. This is evident in many of the policies formulated by the WB and the IMF. It is worth noting that, the 'WTO enables only 25 countries to provide export subsidies for their agricultural products and commodities'[10]. Other countries, which do not have agricultural export subsidies like India, cannot make any new provisions for it. While developing nations are urged to drastically reduce the subsidies, developed nations continue their statusquo.

> Clever manipulation of their subsidies reduction commitment has in reality increased the support to farmers in the developed countries. In the United States, subsidy to a mere 900,000 farmers has increased by 700 times since 1996. Two year before, President Bill Clinton left the office; the US has provided an additional $24 billion to its farmers. The US has rushed to provide an additional $180 billion subsidy over the next 10 years. It claims these are within the limits agreed at the WTO. In absolute terms, the farm support in the 30 richest trading countries had reached to a staggering of $360 billion in 1998. India provides only one billion dollar of indirect subsidies to more than 550 million farmers. In realty India is committed to do away with agricultural subsidies[11].

These are undoubtedly pointers to the partisan attitude of the international institutions in promoting the interest of

---

[10] *Ibid.*, **28**.
[11] *Op.cit.*, **31**.

the developed nations under the disguise of 'helping the third world' nations. The meeting held as part of the decisions taken at the Doha Round was mainly to finalise details about cuts in tariff or industrial products by the developing countries and reduction in agricultural subsidies by the developed countries. Strangely, the US and the European Union while refusing to cut farm subsidies being given to their farmers, insisted on more market accessibility for their industrial products in developing countries by cutting the tariffs there. Clearly the stand taken by the US and the EU was to safeguard the interests of farmers and industrialists in their countries. Undoubtedly, it would be ruinous to the interests of both agricultural farmers and industrial entrepreneurs in developing countries. A 1999 FAO study of 16 countries finds that the WTO's Agreement on Agriculture has led to a surge of food imports but not to an increase in exports[12]. In spite of being a strong protagonist of trade liberalisation, Indian Prime Minister Manmohan Singh opined that, "If trade is to be an instrument of combating poverty and spreading manufacturing capacities more evenly in the world, it is vital that barriers to the export of agricultural goods from developing countries be eliminated"[13]. Developing countries need to negotiate greater access to export markets.

c. Subsidies, Removal of QRs and the Indian Scenario

The Uruguay Round removed or severely curtailed the developing countries' space or ability to provide subsidies

---

[12] John Madeley, *Food for All: Can Hunger be Halved?* (London: The Panos Institute, 2001), 34.

[13] Manmohan Singh, "Towards an Inclusive Globalization", in *The Hindu*, Friday, October 13, 2006. (Excerpted from the Prime Minister's speech at the University Of Cambridge on October 11 on the occasion of his being awarded the honorary degree of Doctor of Law).

for local industries and to maintain some investment measures such as requiring that investors use a minimum level of local materials in their production[14]. This could affect the viability of local firms and sectors. The AoA[15] aims at limiting, if not removing all productions and market distorting interventions like subsidies, protective measures such as quantitative restriction and high tariffs.

> The AoA has three basic components, viz. market access, domestic support and export subsidy. Market access aims at freeing imports from quantitative restrictions and introduction of tariffs with specified upper bounds. Domestic support aims at reducing domestic subsidies to farmers and export subsidy intends to reduce government subsidies to agricultural exports[16].

The agriculture agreement has severe negative effects on many Third World countries. Most of them will have to reduce domestic subsidies to farmers and remove non-tariff controls on agricultural products, converting these to tariffs and then progressively reducing these tariffs. This will impose global competition on the domestic farm sector and threaten the viability of small farms that are unable to compete with cheaper imports. It is noted that the liberalisation policies and the reduction in subsidies together constituted to larger imports which resulted in the reduction of prices and the collapse of local economies in India. The most important impact of liberalisation in agriculture has been the rising indebtedness of the Indian

---

[14] Martin Khor, *Rethinking Globalization* (Bangalore: Books for Change, 2001), 39.

[15] Along with the ongoing process of technical transformation, agriculture has witnessed veritable institutional changes, the most important of which is the liberalized agriculture trade regime characterized by the Agreement on Agriculture (AoA) under the World Trade Organization.

[16] V.P.Ragahavan, "Agricultural Trade Policy and Food Security in India: Issues and Challenges", in *Social Action* (New Delhi: A Social Action Trust Publication, January-March, Vol: 56, No.1) 4.

farmer, which is clearly linked to the changing agricultural policies and priorities, according to the dictates of Structural Adjustment programmes of the World Bank/ IMF combine and the Agreement on Agriculture of the WTO.

Quantitative restrictions (QRs) too are part of the WTO agreements. As per the WTO Agreement on Agriculture, the member countries, both developing and developed are obliged to gradually open up their agricultural sectors to world trade by removing all the trade distortions. Removal of the QRs has major impacts on the agricultural scenario in India.

> Out of the 715 items for which QRs have been lifted from 1st April 2001, 147 items are agricultural and dairy products. The removal of QRs on agricultural commodities makes them vulnerable to global market prices and global competition. Global commodity prices are extremely volatile and in any case do not represent true competition on the basis of production costs, because these markets are controlled by global traders like Cargill who receive overt and covert government subsidies from both exporting and importing governments. The unrestricted access to the Indian market given to the US through the US-India deal on unrestricted imports will threaten the lives and livelihoods of farmers, weavers, retailers and workers in every sector[17].

The Quantitative Restrictions have been removed at the time when the agricultural crisis created by farmer's debt, removal of subsidies, corporate seed failures is forcing thousands of farmers to suicide in Punjab, Andhra Pradesh, Karnataka, Maharashtra and other parts of the country[18]. The removal of QRs has undoubtedly

---

[17] Vandana Shiva, Radha Holla Bharr & Afsar H Jafri, *Corporate Hijack of Agriculture* (New Delhi: Navdanya, 2002,) 6.

[18] *Ibid.,* 6.

aggravated the plight of the farmers in almost all states of India.

d. Regulated Subsidies and its Impacts in India

Subsidies, according to the proponents of globalisation, are regulated in order to give a lending hand to the developing nations. According to them, as the Indian farmers are given a 'negative subsidy', any unfair advantage these farmers get in international markets will be removed. Moreover, as the cost of production in developing countries is far below that of the developed countries, Third World farmers will benefit[19]. In the Agreement on Agriculture(AoA), a section states about domestic support or reduction of domestic subsidies; which states that all support to farmers for food production-support for purchase of seeds, agricultural chemical, for power, for maintaining a minimum support price to ensure farmers' survival, as well as food procurement for public distribution system to ensure that all people get access to affordable food, are deemed to be "trade distorting subsidies" to farmers, and have to be stopped[20]. However the industrialised countries have ensured that they do not have to drastically alter their subsidy structure. While GATT proposals demand the stoppage of subsidies to farmers which are not direct payments, they say nothing about subsidies to corporations that deal with agri-chemicals and grain trade. Between 1995 and 2004, Europe alone has been able to increase its agricultural exports by 26 percent, much of it because of the massive domestic

---

[19] Vandana Shiva, Afsar.H.Jafri and Kunwar Jalees, eds., *The Mirage of Market Access* (New Delhi: Navadanya Research Foundation for Science, Technology and Ecology, 2003), 14.

[20] Vandana Shiva, Radha Holla Bharr and Afsar H Jafri... 2.

and export subsidies that it provides[21]. India's farm imports have meanwhile gone up by 300 percent in volume[22]. According to Vandana Shiva, in 1991, when the Dunkel Draft Text of the GATT Agreement was finalised, we had predicted that given the high subsidies to rich farmers in rich countries, and given the power of global corporations, trade liberalisation of agriculture would be a death knell for Indian farmers[23]. Eight years after the coming into the force of the WTO, poor peasants are being annihilated by the policies and rules of globalisation and their livelihood and incomes are being eroded and in extreme cases their very lives are being extinguished[24].

e. Patent Acts

Patents in the context of agriculture and food production involve ownership over life forms and life processes. Monopoly ownership of life creates an unprecedented crisis for agricultural and food security, by transforming biological resources from common into commodities[25]. It is vital to note how the monopoly-corporatist agenda is ensued through government machineries and policy-making. In order to safe guard the corporate interests, and on the pretext of globalisation, Indian Patent Acts are revised. Corporate monopolies in vital sectors including methods of agriculture and plants had been kept out of the 1970 Indian Patent Act in order to ensure that food and healthcare were affordable and accessible for all,

---

[21] Devinder Sharma, "What Should India Do?", in (Deccan Herald, June 16, 2001), 10.

[22] Ibid., 10.

[23] Vandana Shiva, Afsar.H.Jafri and Kunwar Jalees, eds....5.

[24] Ibid., 5.

[25] Vandana Shiva, Monocultures of the Mind (Dehradun: Natraj Publishers, 1993), 121.

especially the poor and the seed, the first link in the food chain, was held as a common property resource in the public domain[26]. Agriculture plants, seeds, life forms were excluded from patentability and medicines could only be covered by process patents, not product patents[27]. In this manner, it guaranteed farmers the inalienable right to save, exchange and improve upon the seed was not violated.

Nevertheless on 26th of December 2005, the Government of India introduced a Patent Ordinance which threatens to tear down the entire fabric of food security and health security the nation had built carefully and democratically since independence, by creating patent monopolies for seeds and medicines. Recently, two amendments have been made in the 1970 Patent Act. The 2nd Amendment makes changes in the definition of what is NOT an invention. This has opened the flood gates for the patenting of genetically engineered seeds. According to Section 3(j) of the Indian Patent Act, the following is not an invention: Any process for the medical, surgical, creative, prophylactic or other treatment of human beings or any process for a similar treatment of animals or plants or render them free of disease or to increase their economic value or that of their products. In the 2nd Amendment however, the mention of "plants" have been deleted from this section. This deletion implies that a method or process modification of a plant can now be counted as an invention and therefore can be patented. Thus the method of producing Bt. cotton by introducing genes of a bacterium thurengerisis in cotton to produce toxins to kill the bollworm can now be covered by the exclusive rights associated with patents. In other words, Monsanto can now have Bt. cotton patents in India. The Second Amendment has also added a new section 3(j). This section allows for the production or propagation of genetically

[26] *www.zmag.org*, downloaded on 31.01.2007.

[27] *www.zmag.org*, downloaded on 31.01.2007.

engineered plants to count as an invention. This section excludes as inventions "plants and animals in whole or any part thereof other than microorganisms but including seeds, varieties and species and essentially biological processes for production of propagation of plants and animals". The clause thus introduces patents on life forms. Since "microorganism has not been clearly defined, it leaves the term to cover cells, cell-lines, genes etc. Further by using the qualifier "essentially biological processes", it opens the flood gates for patenting of genetically engineered plants and animals. The clause should have only started "plants and animals" will not be patentable. Since plants produced through the use of new biotechnologies are not technically considered "essentially biological," section 3j has found another way to create room for Monsanto's monopolies. What is most concerning is how the language of section 3j is a verbatim translation into India law of Article 27.3 (b) of TRIPS Agreement. Article 27.3 (b) of TRIPS states: Parties may exclude from patentability plants and animals other than micro-organisms, and essentially biological processes for the production of plants and animals other than non-biological and microbiological processes. However, parties shall provide for the protection of plant varieties either by patents or by an effective sui-generis system or by any combination thereof. This provision shall be reviewed four years after the entry into force of the Agreement establishing the W.T.O[28].

Looking with closer analysis, there are three ways that the 2nd Amendment and 3rd Amendment of the Indian Patent laws have jeopardised our seed and food security, and hence our national security. Firstly, it allows patents on seeds and plants through sections 3(i) and 3(j), as we saw above. Patents are monopolies and exclusive rights which prevent farmers from saving seeds; and seed companies from producing seeds.

---

[28] *www.zmag.org*, downloaded on 31.01.2007.

Patents on seeds transform seed saving into an "intellectual property crime". Secondly, when combined with the product patents of the 3rd Amendment, Patents on Life in the 2nd Amendment can mean absolute monopoly. A decision on a plant patent infringement suit has set a new precedent for interpreting plant patent coverage. In the case of Imagio Nursery vs. Daina Greenhouse, Judge Spence Williams, for the U.S. District Court for the Northern District of California, ruled that a plant patent can be infringed by a plant that merely has similar characteristics to the patented plant. When combined with the reversal of burden of proof clauses of TRIPS, this kind of precedence based on product patents can be disastrous for countries from where the biodiversity that gave rise to those properties was first taken. Patent protection implies the exclusion of farmers' right over the resources having these genes and characteristics. This will undermine the very foundations of agriculture[29].

For example, a patent has been granted in the U.S. to a biotechnology company, Sungene, for a sunflower variety with very high oleic acid content. The claim was for the characteristic (i.e. high oleic acid) and not just for the genes producing the characteristic Sungene has notified others involved in sunflower breeding that the development of any variety high in oleic acid will be considered an infringement of its patent. Thus a company can introduce traits through genetic engineering, and then claim monopoly on the trait even in traditional varieties through a product patent. A product patent in effect says that it does not matter how a property was created, came into existence, whether a result of evolution, or farmers breeding, or genetic pollution is patent infringement and theft. Our saline resistant rices, our high protein wheats are all vulnerable to biopiracy through product patents. And our farmers are liable to be sued for piracy if farmers rights are not explicitly protected in future amendments of the Patent

---

[29] *Ibid.*

law. Thirdly, genetic pollution is inevitable. Monsanto will use the patents and pollution to claim ownership of crops on farmers' fields where the Bt. gene has reached it through wind or pollinators. This has been established as precedence in the case of a Canadian farmer, Percy Schmeiser, whose canola field was contaminated by Monsanto's "Round up Ready Canola," but instead of Monsanto demanded $200,000 fine for "theft" of Monsanto's "intellectual property". Thousands of U.S. farmers also have been sued for contaminated crops. Will Indian farmers be blamed for theft when Monsanto's GM cotton contaminates their crops? Or will the government wake up and enforce strict monitoring and liability? In countries, where plant patents are not allowed, patenting genes is available as an opening for patenting properties and characteristics of the plant, and hence having exclusive rights to those properties and characteristics[30].

India, in its discussion paper submitted to the TRIPS Council stated: "Patenting of life forms may have at least two dimensions. Firstly, there is the ethical question of the extent of private ownership that could be extended to life forms. The second dimension relates to the use of IPRs' concept as understood in the industrialised world and its appropriateness in the face of the larger dimension of rights on knowledge, their ownership, use, transfer and dissemination".

f. Contract Farming and Traditional Farmers

Contract farming is a novel way of employing farmers to reap profits for the corporate giants and this is said to have pushed aside traditional farmers, thereby converting their soil into deep catastrophe. Contract farming implies that the farmer has to sell the produce to the corporation at a price determined exclusively by corporate and trade monopolies and not by farmers. Contract farming is taking

---

[30] *Op.cit.*

place in two sectors: for multinationals in the agro-processing industry and for the seed industry[31]. According to Vandana Shiva, in the Contract Agreement of Bioseed Research India Pvt. Ltd., there are many clauses that are detrimental to farmers. For her, "The contracts usually made with illiterate farmers, is usually one-sided, where the farmer is held liable for carrying out the entire production, paying wages, meeting fertiliser and pesticide costs, as well as ensuring that' a minimum of (specified) kilometer isolation distance is maintained from the nearest field planted with the same crop"[32]. The contract also states that the company reserves the right to reject the crop in case the quality standards are not met by the producer or even if the harvested seed is damaged and becomes qualitatively unacceptable due to rains or disease[33]. Moreover the farmer is not allowed to sell the seed outside; he/she has to sell it to the company as grain. Contract farming for the agro-processing industry means a shift away from food crops to cash crops, further weakening food security. The greatest criticism against contract farming is that the crop and the variety to be planted will be determined by the corporation not on the grounds of ensuring food for the people, rather on ground of profitability. Traditional farmers are thus reduced to 'workers' dependent on corporations for their survival.

g. New Seed Policies and the Threat of Super Weeds

Subsequent changes following the patent acts, new seed policies are formulated which resulted in casting out

---

[31] Vandana Shiva, *Gloablisation of Agriculture* (New Delhi: Research Foundation for Science, Technology and Ecology, 2000), 48.

[32] *Ibid.*, 48.

[33] Quoted by Vandana Shiva in Vandana Shiva, *Globalization of Agriculture* (New Delhi: Research Foundation for Science, Technology and Ecology, 2000), 48.

traditional seeds and allowing the Super weeds and monopolies to dominate. According to Henk Hobbelink, "Patented varieties would make it illegal for farmers to use part of their harvest for next years' sowing as the germplasm in the seeds would continue to be owned by the patentee. The farmer would have to return to the market each year to purchase seed as is now the case with hybrid crops. It would also be illegal for a farmer to pass on harvested seed to his neighbors or sell it on a limited scale"[34]. "The result of the extended property protection would be to increase greatly the farming community's dependence on the plant breeding and biotechnology industry. It would also mean the total loss of the genetic diversity that is maintained in the field by farmers through the election and use of their own seed"[35]. Biotechnological giants like Monsanto and others claim monopoly on plant breeding and they sell very expensive seeds which require heavy agricultural input, besides; the farmers have no right to reuse them for further sowing or crossbreeding[36]. According to Richard Hindmarsh, "The ultimate danger of increased reliance on corporate-DNA crop regime is that eventually there will be few alternatives to genetically engineered seed. Farmers who want to use bromoxynil as a cotton herbicide will have to buy a 'package' of bromoxynil and bromoxynil-tolerant cotton seeds from Rhone-Poulene- a major manufacturer of bromoxynil and leading international seed manufacturer. On the other hand, farmers who want to buy open pollinated seed will find it increasingly hard to do so.

---

[34] Bharat Dogra, *Seeds Industry of India: Seeds Of Plenty or Seeds of Discontent* (New Delhi: Navdanya & NFS-India, 1993), 45.

[35] Bharat Dogra... 45.

[36] Robert Ali Brac De La Perriere & Franck Seuret (eds), *Brave New Seeds: The Threat of GM Crops To Farmers* (London: Zed Books, 2000), 8.

Consequently the current trend of farmers switching to ecological methods of farming like permaculture, organic and biodynamic farming, could be seriously retarded"[37]. The Parliamentary Standing Committee has found that the dependency of the farmers on private companies for seeds is greater than ever and this situation is being exploited by the multinational companies to reap profits[38]. Since the private sector is encouraged to have greater share in the agriculture sector, The Parliamentary Standing Committee noted that this leads farmers to a grave situation and thus suggested that the 'Plant Protection of Varieties and Farmers Rights' act be implemented and public sector should continue to have the key role in seed policies[39]. The Parliamentary Standing Committee has also pointed out that Monsanto; an MNC has sold the cotton weeds for a very huge profit and thus recommended the parliament to include a seed price regulatory clause in the bill to be presented in the parliament[40]. The grave situation of farmers being denied access to seeds and corporations monopolising and reaping profits is thus reflected in farmers in the third world raising the slogan, "Seeds belong to farmers and not to corporations. Farmers have always protected the broad diversity of their fields"[41]. The empirical reality of the impact of the liberalisation of the seed sector is an epidemic of suicides linked to high debts for purchase of seeds, agrichemicals and pesticides[42].

---

[37] Bharat Dogra... 45.

[38] V.Jain, "Vithu Bill Karshaka Thatparyam Samrakshikkanam-Parliamentary Samithy" in *Deshabhimani Daily,* 29.11.2006.

[39] *Ibid.*

[40] *Ibid.*

[41] Robert Ali Brac De La Perriere & Franck Seuret (eds)... 7.

[42] Vandana Shiva, *Globalization of Agriculture Food Security and Sustainability* (New Delhi: Research Foundation for Science, Technology and Ecology, 1999), 43.

h. Displacement of Third World Farmers

It is generally implicit that although, displacement of farmers is not a new phenomenon and was already seen at the beginning of the first Green revolution in the 1960's and 1970's, there have been a considerably increased percentage of farmers being displaced after the initiation of globalisation. 'Every increase in the degree of complexity of agricultural practices, with the global liberalisation of exchange, has caused a phenomenon of concentration of agricultural production owing to which bigger and more modern farmers have absorbed smaller farms, sending millions of rural folk towards big cities'[43]. 'The complexity of the techniques implemented, their degree of technicality, and their cost can only accelerate the marginalisation of small-scale farmers all over the world'[44]. The escalating displacement is due to import policies that influence prices, decline in productivity even after the usage of genetic seeds, increased expenditure and cutting down of subsidies. The International People's Tribunal to judge the G-7 Tokyo, July, 1993 stated that, "almost one-third of all cereals consumed are imported from abroad in several countries burdened with SAPs and in the Carribean and parts of Latin America, food self-reliance is on the decline; in 1991-92 in India, the production of cash crops for export rose 3%, while the cultivation of basic grains fell 1.5% as the country's SAP got underway"[45]. A study conducted by "Friends of Earth", an international organisation, found that farmers in the U.S, Argentina, China, Paraguay, Uruguay, Canada,

---

[43] Robert Ali Brac De La Perriere & Franck Seuret (eds)... 13.

[44] *Ibid.,* 13.

[45] *The People vs Global Capital: The G-7, TNC's, SAP's and Human Rights,* Report of the International People's Tribunal to Judge the G-7, Tokyo, July 1993 (Japan: PARC, 1994), 146.

Brazil and India where genetic seeds are being used for agricultural production could not make any benefits out of the genetic seeds that were started using from 1996-2006[46]. Nevertheless companies like Monsanto made huge profits during this period. In 2004 genetic seeds were cultivated in 17.5 crore acres of land in which 91% of the seeds used were bought from Monsanto[47]. It was also noted in the study that the traditional farmers in China produced better results than those who used genetic seeds. Moreover pesticides used in those lands were higher by 20%. While 5.7 dollars was spend for pesticides in the traditional farms, 16.01dollars was spend for pesticides on a hectare of genetically cultivated lands[48]. It was explored that in India, the expenses were comparatively lesser in traditional farming lands. While only ₹ 9653 was spend on traditional farming methods, ₹ 10,655 was spend on farms that used genetically modified seeds[49]. Furthermore, when traditional seeds produced upto 690 kilograms of cotton weeds from an acre, genetically modified seeds could generate only 450 kilograms of produce[50]. It was found that those farmers who relied on genetically modified seeds had to bear losses upto ₹ 6663 per acre[51]. It was also the reason behind suicidal deaths reported in Maharashtra, and Andhra where huge losses were suffered by the farmers. It was also noted in the study that the traditional farmers in China produced better results than those who used genetic seeds. Moreover pesticides used in those lands were higher by 20%. While

---

[46] V. Jain, *Deshabhimani Daily,* 31.01.2007, 2.

[47] *Ibid.,* 2.

[48] V. Jain, *Deshabhimani Daily,* 31.01.2007, 2.

[49] *Ibid.,* 2.

[50] *Ibid.,* 2.

[51] *Ibid.,* 2.

5.7 dollars was spend for pesticides in the traditional farms, 16.01dollars was spend for pesticides on a hectare of genetically cultivated lands[52]. The indictment signed by the International People's Tribunal to judge the G-7 Tokyo, July, 1993 stated that the liberalisation process initiated through Structural Adjustment Policies, "lead to the displacement of small-scale agricultural producers through the lowering of external tariffs and entry of highly subsidised agricultural imports, the removal of subsidies for farm inputs, the reduction of credit and a rise in interest rates, and an emphasis on export production at the expenses of subsistence farming and staple food producers"[53] Peasants are being pushed off the land and their uprooting is being facilitated by policies that are transferring rural capital from farming communities to private investors[54].

i. Poverty and Debt Crisis

According to Vandana Shiva, the second important impact that happened along with the centralisation of agriculture was debt. For her, just the borrowing of the first round of IDB credits leading to the IBRD in the Green Revolution stage increased our foreign debt five-fold, just for chemicals for agriculture. As a result of Structural Adjustment measures introduced in 1991, the total debt of India had increased from ₹ 280,746 crore in 1992-93 to ₹ 429,271 crore in 2000[55]. However it is argued that there are debt

---

[52] Ibid., 2.

[53] The People vs Global Capital: The G-7, TNC's, SAP's and Human Rights, Report of the International People's Tribunal to Judge the G-7, Tokyo, July 1993 (Japan: PARC, 1994), 132.

[54] Vandana Shiva, Globalization of Agriculture and the Growth of Food Insecurity, (New Delhi: Research Foundation for Science, Technology and Natural Resource Policy, 1996), 15.

[55] Vandana Shiva, Radha Holla Bharr & Afsar H Jafri, Corporate Hijack of Agriculture (New Delhi: Navdanya, 2002,) 3.

relief measures to assist debtor nations. Nevertheless, as Oxfam has pointed out, under the Enhanced Heavily Indebted Poor Countries (HIPC) Initiative, 26 countries are receiving debt relief, but half of them are still spending 15 percent or more of government revenue on debt repayments[56]. Thirteen of the twenty six countries receiving debt relief are still spending more on repaying debt than on others[57]. Thus debts impose a major burden on poor nations with crippling short- and long-term effects on economic management[58]. Debts encapsulate the culmination of dues stemming from inability to manage domestic-external relationships[59]. Activists from across Africa and Asia gathered on the opening weekend of the World Social Forum to plan stronger Afro-Asia links between social movements in their fight against globalisation and raised the slogan, "You(Bush) say drop bomb, we say drop the debt", writes Shafqat Munir[60]. According to a report presented in a Press conference, the Chief Minister of Kerala stated that 1500 farmers in Kerala have committed suicide due to falling prices and debts[61]. *Five more debt trapped farmers have committed suicide in different parts of rural Vidarbha in Maharashtra, taking the toll to 67 in January alone. Three of the five farmers who ended their lives on Tuesday belonged to the most distressed Yavatmal district of western Vidarbha while the other two*

---

[56] Larry Elliot, "Stop the recycled peanuts to Africa", in *Deccan Herald*, Friday, August 2, 2002

[57] *Ibid.*, 10

[58] Sumit Roy, *Globalization, ICT and Developing Nations* (New Delhi: Sage Publications, 2005,), 83.

[59] *Ibid.*, 83.

[60] *People's Reporter*, Vol. 20, Issue 2, January 25- February 10, (Mumbai: 2007), 5.

[61] *www.deshabhimani.com/news/k5.htm*, downloaded on 14.07.2006.

were from Akola and Bhandara on the eastern side of the region. Eleven farmers had killed themselves I the preceding two days. The 16 suicides in the last 72 hours show that the trend continues even in the post harvest season amid government claims of large-scale disbursement of relief. The relatively lower scale of suicides in the first month of the New Year compared to the rate of over 100 suicides a month in 2006 has been cited by Amaravati divisional commissioner S.K.Goyal as an indication that the relief packages were working well. Kishor Tiwari, leader of the VJAS[62], however refuted the government claims. Reiterating the demand for adequate budgetary allocation for agriculture, which stands at a meager four percent and fundamental changes in the farm policy, Tiwari said he would impress upon MP's the need to build pressure on the government to achieve it. The other demands Tiwari proposes to lobby for during his visit to New Delhi are declaring Vidarbha an organic farming zone as recommended by the National Commission for Farmers, hike in import duty on cotton and fillip to rural health infrastructure[63].

j. Indian Agriculture Economy into Peril

Globalisation of agriculture is said to have integrated international agriculture market assisting the third world agriculture economies towards progress. Indian Agriculture Sector however has a different story to narrate in spite of whatever it has achieved through the globalising process according to its proponents. Apart from making farmers dependent on high cost external inputs, agricultural intensification led to the loss of agro-biodiversity and the marginalisation of several important

---

[62] Vidarbha Jan Andolan Samiti.
[63] *Malayala Manorama* Daily, 01.02.2007, 6.

local crops and crop varieties[64]. The indictment signed by the International People's Tribunal to judge the G-7 Tokyo, July, 1993 stated that the liberalisation process initiated through Structural Adjustment Policies, "lead to the displacement of small-scale agricultural producers through the lowering of external tariffs and entry of highly subsidised agricultural imports, the removal of subsidies for farm inputs, the reduction of credit and a rise in interest rates, and an emphasis on export production at the expenses of subsistence farming and staple food producers"[65]. Indian farmers had to pay a huge price for what is termed to be the development agenda initiated as part of the globalising process. It is reported that there are 20,000 farm suicides and 20,000 starvation deaths and 5 million farm livelihood lost[66]. Data, below-stated clearly indicates how globalisation is contributive to increased poverty due to falling prices and disappearing income in India[67].

Crops	Per Year
Oilseeds	₹ 20 billion (₹ 25, 000 crore)
Potato	₹ 50 billion (₹ 5,000 crore)
Sugarcane	₹ 15 billion (₹ 1,500 crore)
Wheat	₹ 210 billion (₹ 21,000 crore)
Rice	₹ 270 billion (₹ 27,000 crore)

---

[64] N.S.Jodha, *Sustainable Development in Fragile Environments* (Ahmedabad: Centre for Environment Education, 1995), 80.

[65] *The People vs Global Capital: The G-7, TNC's, SAP's and Human Rights,* Report of the International People's Tribunal to Judge the G-7, Tokyo, July 1993, (Japan: PARC, 1994), 132.

[66] Vandana Shiva, Afsar.H.Jafri and Kunwar Jalees, eds., *The Mirage Of Market Access* (New Delhi: Navadanya Research Foundation for Science, Technology and Ecology, 2003), 3.

[67] *Ibid.*, 3.

Crops	Per Year
Milk	₹ 340 billion (₹ 34,000 crore)
Tea	₹ 21 billion (₹ 2,100 crore)
Spices and plantation crops in Kerala	₹ 1 billion (₹ 100 crore)
Failure of Monsanto's Corn in Bihar	₹ 4 billion (₹ 400 crore)
Failure of Bt Corn in India (seven states)	₹ 1 billion (₹ 100 crore)
Total	**₹ 1162 billion (116200 crores)**
In US dollars	**$ 26000 million**

And these losses are in just a few crops and a few states, which Research Foundation for Science, Technology and Ecology has monitored. Declining farm incomes also impact the rest of the economy due to loss of purchasing power. Since 75% of India is rural this increase in poverty in rural India translates into a chain reaction throughout the economy[68].

It was expected that with the removal of trade distortion measures agricultural exports from the developing countries would increase, which did not happen. In fact, India has on the other hand seen a massive increase in the imports of agricultural products and commodities from about ₹ 5000 crore in 1995 to over ₹ 15000 crore in 2000 a three-fold increase[69].

India as a nation faces many challenges in the present context. Growth is envisioned in all sectors through liberalisation policies. Amidst this, mass poverty,

---

[68] Vandana Shiva, Afsar.H.Jafri and Kunwar Jalees, eds., *The Mirage of Market Access* (New Delhi: Navadanya Research Foundation for Science, Technology and Ecology, 2003), 3.

[69] *Ibid.,* 28.

unemployment, population growth etc. are some of the realities that need to be dealt with. Agricultural growth envisioned through opening up economy, revised policies and biotechnological innovations are believed to elevate the status of the poor and supportive in combating poverty. However the above analysis is an apparent evidence that globalisation of agriculture exerts high pressure on the developed as well as the developing and third world nations world wide and particularly an agrarian economy like India. This process not only exerts pressure, rather push aside predominantly agrarian economies like India into peril. In spite of being assured the integration and exchange of knowledge resources though the process of globalisation, it is evident that the economically powerful are controlling and the global institutions are in the driver's seat as far as globalisation of agriculture is concerned. Mutuality is not the governing principle in the process. Furthermore, developed nations are on a spree to make advantage of the processes of globalisation to reap profits and to ensure safety to their own agriculture sector. This approach challenges the traditional farmers of the third world to confront the ideology and operational principles behind globalisation of agriculture in order to safeguard their rights and access to livelihood. The escalating suicidal deaths of farmers, their displacements and debts are pointers to a ruined economy struggling to respond to a vast population dependent on agriculture to sustain their livelihood.

Social Implications - Case Study

Wayanad is chosen as a case to evaluate the impact of globalisation in one of the geographically smallest states of India, Kerala. Wayanad being selected for this study is in view of the fact that, the writer hails from Kerala and has been carefully watching the developments and got interested in some of the people's movements emerged in solidarity with the people of Wayanad. Wayanad is one of the Northern districts of Kerala comprising a considerable number of 'adivasi[70]' population. There are also a considerable number of migrants from the central and other parts of Kerala who came and settled mostly after World War II to this beautiful little Adivasi region on the North-Eastern tip of the State. With its cash crops of pepper, coffee, cardamom, tea and spices, this district has been one of the biggest foreign exchange earners of Kerala. However, Wayanad registers the largest number of farmer suicidal deaths in the State.

Price Crash, Debts and Suicides

The rapid decline of the economy in this once rich cash-crop district reverberates across the spectrum. The crisis, of which the price fall has been one major part, has sparked off many suicides. Small and marginal farmers have been devastated. The district secretary of N. Surendran of Indian Farmers Movement (INFAM) says, "Yes drought and disease hurt us. And this high-pesticide chemical farming model must go. But it is these free trade policies that have driven prices down". Price rigging, the dumping of imports and crop failure have proved a lethal mix. "Foreign and domestic corporate and trade cartels are behind the price crash, says P.A. Muhammad, convener of the South Indian Farmers Co-ordination Committee (SIFCO). Those in coffee, pepper and tea in this district, he points out; have suffered a loss of at least ₹ 1,003 crores a year since 2001. On pepper alone, cultivators have lost ₹ 1500 crores since that year. According to Fr. Vettikattil, we got just Rs. 50,000 from those 90 acres. In better times, that should have been 20

---

[70] Tribals are known as 'Adivasis' in Kerala.

lakhs. By March this year "every acre of land in the Mullankolly-Pulpally region carried a debt of ₹ 2 lakh to ₹ 3 lakh", says M.Prakash of the Brahmagiri development Society. "The price crash had made repayment of loans impossible", he points out and the five-fold drop in the price of pepper was a huge blow. Quick wilt disease enhanced its impact. Growing debt, says Prakash, forced many to fell countless trees on their lands to sell the timber. In this ecologically fragile zone, that only doubled the damage. The collapse of coffee prices has ruined countless farmers in the district, says M.P.Veerendrakumar who represents Wayanad in the Lok Sabha. "So many lives are tied to that crop", he says. There are over 70,000 hectares under coffee here and some 60,000 small growers. The slide in prices is a key element in the farmers' suicides that have occurred. For him, the retail prices are not doing badly but it is the producer's prices that have plummeted. Coffee prices dropped to a low of ₹ 15-16 a kg for the raw cherry and this from a high of ₹ 70-80 a kg for the cherry and up to ₹ 130 a kg for the beans only a few years ago. 'This place is drowning in third-rate imported pepper; cheap, low grade imports are killing our pepper. This massive inflow has savaged the growers here and knocked the bottom of out of the districts' economy'. Wayanad farmers have lost ₹ 1,500 crore on pepper alone since 2001, says P.A.Muhammed, convenor of the South Indian Farmers Coordination Committee. According to Samad, 'The import lobby brings in these large amounts of bad pepper and it mixes with Wayanad pepper and exports it to Europe and elsewhere for huge profits. This triggered the price crash and killed farmers of Wayanad'.

Chapter 3

ANALYSIS OF VANDANA SHIVA'S ADVOCACY OF SUSTAINABLE AGRICULTURE

1. Introduction

It should be acknowledged that globalisation has brought about significant changes globally, in which a few have produced positive results. However agriculture sector in India after the advent of globalising process has witnessed many setbacks and needs to be critically evaluated. Analysis in the former chapter makes it clear that traditional farming methods and traditional farmers are in doldrums and the policies in order to facilitate agriculture growth are derogatory in nature in spite of a number of progresses envisioned through globalisation. Moreover food security has given way to food productivity and profitability. These significant changes also need to be evaluated in the light of escalating farmer suicide deaths and increasing poverty and debt rates. Hence a sustainable, farmer friendly and food security enabling paradigm needs to be evolved in order to enhance the livelihood of the people of our nation.

Vandana Shiva is a world-renowned activist who is deeply involved in developing an alternative system that would enhance sustainability. She is a physicist, philosopher and activist, who was born in the city of Dehradun, located at the bottom of Himalayas. She holds a master's degree in particle physics and in 1978 completed her Ph.D. in the philosophy of science. Dr.

Shiva founded the *Navdanya* system of agriculture that conserves agricultural diversity. It places the farmer at the center of conservation and empowers him/her to take control over the political, ecological and economic aspects of agriculture. In 1991 she founded *Navdanya*, a national movement to protect the diversity and integrity of living resources, especially native seeds. Dr. Shiva has contributed in fundamental ways to changing the practice and paradigms of agriculture and food. Her books, "The Violence of Green Revolution" and "Monocultures of the Mind" have become basic challenges to the dominant paradigm of non-sustainable, reductionist Green revolution Agriculture. Demystifying GATT, working with farmers to explain TRIPS and the Agreement of Agriculture are other dimensions of her work on Agriculture and Food Security. The "Neem Campaign" and "Basmati Campaign" are other examples of her leadership in IPR and Biopiracy issues. Besides her activism, she also serves on expert groups of government on IPR legislation.

2. What is Sustainable-Growth Paradigm?

Much of the debate about the future of agriculture revolves around different approaches to farming. Is it best for food production to use the latest science and technology to boost productivity, control pests and respond to the demands of the international market, or to use fewer chemicals and pesticides? Should farming be on a large scale or a small one? There are different approaches taken in regard to these questions. One of the approaches is to bring in agriculture into the gamut of economic category. The orthodox economic opinion since early 1980's has been that maximising international trade reduces prices and stimulates economic growth and in this way helps countries raise their standards of living and reduce poverty and by implication, hunger[1]. Many feel that biotechnological advancements and genetic engineering methods should be utilised to boost agricultural growth while others feel that the growth should be sustainable and environment friendly. Within the bandwagon of 'sustainable agriculture' itself there are different operational concepts emerging. Green revolution proponents continue their advocacy of high-tech, chemical agriculture, yet they now feel comfortable in joining the sustainable agriculture bandwagon. From a certain perspective, sustainable agriculture is all related to the question of social justice and of social equity. According to this position, it is terribly unjust for a few people to make profits out of the poverty and oppression of many. For them, earlier, national development projected higher standards of living for people, now globalisation promises a better world for only those who enter the charmed circle of the world market economy. It is contested that this paradigm is premised on neo-liberalism that can only favour those who already have entitlements of wealth and privilege, economic and social capital such as poor and the underprivileged do not possess. Inevitably, according to this view point, such economic globalisation excludes those thus handicapped, and sharpens the economic inequalities and social disparities even further. Moreover, in India, as in other developing countries, this market-friendly economy has reflected and strengthened iniquitous traditional social structures further, and created new and more iniquitous ones.

'Growth' envisioned through biotechnological innovations that increases productivity is yet another

---

[1] John Madeley, *Food for All: Can Hunger be Halved?* (London: The Panos Institute, 2001), 31.

stream of agricultural development paradigm propagated with much rigor and assumes to be a dominant paradigm. What the proponents of biotechnological innovations envisage through the globalising process is pertinent.

> For them, the key contributions of biotechnology will be several fold: producing more food on the same area of land, thereby reducing pressure to expand into wilderness, rainforests or marginal lands which support biodiversity and vital ecosystem services; reducing post-harvest loss of food(caused by disease, pests and decay) and improving the quality of fresh and processed foods, thus boosting the 'realised nutritional yields' per acre; displacing resource- and energy-intensive inputs, such as fuel, fertilisers or pesticides, thus reducing unintended impacts on environment and freeing those resources to be used for other purposes or to be conserved for the future; encouraging reduction of environmentally damaging agricultural practices and adopting more sustainable practices such as conservation tillage, precision agriculture and integrated crop management; stimulation of a new kind of economic growth; more benefits with less input and harm[2].

Those who view biotechnological innovations and genetic engineering methods as engines of growth also profess a genus of 'sustainability'. However, *Vandana Shiva has taken a fundamental position that avows diversity and asserts that sustainability depends on diversity.* For her, *"Sustainable agriculture is based on the sustainable use of natural resources-land water and agricultural biodiversity including plants and animals. The sustainable use of these resources in turn requires that their ownership and control lie with decentralised agricultural communities to generate their livelihoods, provide food and conserve natural resources. These three dimensions*

---

[2] Robert Ali Brac De La Perriere & Franck Seuret (eds), *Brave New Seeds: The Threat of GM Crops To Farmers* (London: Zed Books, 2000), 57.

of ecological security, livelihood security and food security are essential elements of an agriculture policy which is sustainable and equitable"[3]. For Vandana Shiva, "The diversity which is the basis of sustainable agriculture, and that which is being destroyed by monocultures is the key to food security at the domestic and the community level"[4]. She believes that the large scale corporate farms being created for export-oriented floriculture, horticulture and aquaculture are aggravating the non-sustainable use of natural resources which has already been the result of green revolution practices. Vandana Shiva opines that according to the dominant paradigm of production, diversity goes against productivity, which creates an imperative for uniformity and monocultures[5]. She asserts that organic farming and low external input agriculture are being recognised everywhere as necessary for environmental protection, health protection and the protection of food security. According to Vandana Shiva, strengthening sustainable farming, based primarily on diversity and negating monoculture, is therefore, necessary for strengthening food security at both local and national levels. She reinstates that diversity is the characteristic of nature and the basis of ecological stability and sustainability.

a. Illusions of Growth and Dominant Paradigms

There are different development paradigms that evaluate and offer propositions to human development. Green

---

[3] Vandana Shiva, *Globalisation of Agriculture Food Security and Sustainability* (New Delhi: Research Foundation for Science, Technology and Ecology, 1999), 1.

[4] Vandana Shiva, Globalisation of Agriculture and the Growth of Food Insecurity (New Delhi: Research Foundation for Science, Technology and Natural Resource Policy, 1996), 27.

[5] Vandana Shiva, *Monocultures of the Mind* (Dehradun: Natraj Publishers, 1993), 70.

Revolution is being viewed as one such development paradigm that contributed to the agriculture progress of India. Globalisation is perceived to be another form of development agenda that will foster growth in agriculture sector. Nevertheless both these paradigms have brought in sharp criticism. According to Robert Ali Brac De La Perriere and Franck Seuret, in the name of progress and the necessity of increased yields, the Green Revolution enforced a mode of agriculture that had high-yield varieties, fertilisers and pesticides as its new gods[6]. For them (Robert Ali Brac De La Perriere & Franck Seuret), gradually many Indian farmers abandoned the principles of sustainable agriculture and converted to intensive agriculture, relegating four millennia of experience to the limbo of history and all that for a revolution in agriculture sector however didn't live up to its promises[7]. The advent of globalisation is contributive to various new models, especially in the filed of agriculture that is said to be instrumental to growth. According to this dominant paradigm of production, diversity goes against productivity, which creates an imperative for uniformity and monocultures[8]. This for them should be achieved through trade liberalisation and intensive agricultural practices. It should be noted that trade liberalisation policies are based on the theory of comparative advantage. According to Vandana Shiva, on the logic of comparative advantage it is argued that a nation can enhance efficiency in resource

---

[6] Robert Ali Brac De La Perriere & Franck Seuret (eds), *Brave New Seeds: The Threat of GM Crops To Farmers* (London: Zed Books, 2000), 1.

[7] It was noted that the number of hectares cultivated increased; but productivity, which rose in the initial years, progressively declined. Moreover the consumption of fertilizers and pesticides increased enormously and the number of varieties cultivated dropped sharply.

[8] Vandana Shiva, *Monocultures of the Mind...*, 134.

use and hence net welfare, by producing and exporting commodities in which it is relatively efficient, and importing commodities in which it is relatively not so[9]. However in this paradigm of development, living species are seen as 'genetic resources', genes are seen as protein factories, the living being is reduced to the state of an industrial product protected by intellectual property rights[10]. In the dominant paradigm, technology is seen as being above society both in its structure and evolution, in its offering technological fixes, and in its technological determinism[11].

b. Alternative Paradigms

Alternative paradigms that uphold agriculture sustainability as well as ecological conservation and diversity offer a critique mainly to the capitalistic form of development paradigm. A shift from "food first" to "trade first" and "farmer first" to "corporation first" policies appears to be the major thrust of intense capitalistic agriculture trade[12]. Capitalistic economic paradigm, according to its antagonists, ensures only a quantitative increase of values. The critique is that capitalist expansion in pursuit of quantitative growth undermines the ecological processes and reduces their quality and potential to satisfy human needs. Conversely, alternative paradigms stress on qualitative changes and sustainability. While capitalist

---

[9] Vandana Shiva, *Globalisation of Agriculture Food Security and Sustainability* (New Delhi: Research Foundation for Science, Technology and Ecology, 1999), 11.

[10] Robert Ali Brac De La Perriere & Franck Seuret (eds), *Brave New Seeds: The Threat of GM Crops To Farmers* (London: Zed Books, 2000), 20.

[11] Vandana Shiva, "Biotechnological Development and the Conservation of Biodiversity", in Vandana Shiva, Ingunn Moser, eds., *Biopolitics-A Feminist and Ecological Reader in Biotechnology* (London: Zed Books Ltd, 1995), 193.

[12] *www.zmag.org*, downloaded on 31.01.2007.

rationality is measured by the profit rates, ecologically-alert rationality emphasises the significance of mutual existence. Vandana Shiva cites an example to elaborate the two different attitudes towards a common problem: Pests. For her, pests are a product of a disharmony within plants and in ecosystems. *Weaving harmony in sustainable agriculture implies bringing back the diversity which creates pest - predator balance and organic methods of breeding and production which produce resilient plants. However, in the dominant paradigm of agriculture, pests are not seen a product of disharmony but as reductionist, essentialised, absolutised undesirable entities which must be exterminated with the most potent and toxic methods. While pests are not a problem in ecologically balanced agriculture, in an unstable agricultural system, they pose a serious challenge to agronomy. The metaphor for pesticide use in agriculture then becomes a war while sustainable methods strive to bring back the harmony[13].* Certain ecological thinkers and activists are unhappy with the shallow reforms aimed at preserving the nature. Hence they have taken a radical approach known as 'deep ecology' formulated by Naess[14]. According to Naess this basic position is marked by the "eight points of deep ecology"[15]:

1. The well being and flourishing of human and non-human life on earth have a value in themselves, independently of their usefulness for human purposes.

---

[13] *www.zmag.org*, downloaded on 31.01.2007.

[14] The Norwegain philosopher Arne Naess coined this terminology in the early 70's and it has evolved into an ideology which guides many eco-activists, especially in North America.

[15] Bas Wielenga, *Towards an Eco-Just Society* (Bangalore: Centre for Social Action, 1999), 118.

2. Richness and diversity of life-forms are also values in themselves.

3. Humans have no right to reduce this richness and diversity to satisfy vital needs.

4. The flourishing of human life is compatible with a smaller human population. The flourishing of non-human life also requires a smaller human population.

5. The present human interference with the non-human world is excessive.

6. Policies must therefore be basically changed.

7. Appreciating life quality has to replace adhering to ever higher standards of living.

8. Those who subscribe to these points have an obligation to try to implement them.

The basic intention of the deep ecologists is to identify the deeper roots of the eco-crisis and to address them through a transformation of the relationship between humans and nature[16]. Within the deep ecology movement different tendencies have evolved. The "Earth First" movement in the USA represents a form of radical biocentrism, which reverses the subjugation of humans under nature[17].

c. Framework of Sustainability

In spite of the concept of sustainability being variously formulated, the central notion in most definitions and formulations is the issue of inter-generational equity or the idea that each generation is responsible in dealing with the nature and its resources so as to ensure the

---

[16] *Ibid.*

[17] *Ibid.*, 119.

welfare prospects of future generations[18]. *"Sustainability is the ability of a system (e.g. fragile resource agriculture) to maintain a certain well-defined level of performance (output) over time, and if required, to enhance the same in response to changing needs, either by itself or through linkages with other systems, without damaging the long-term productivity of its resource base and the essential ecological integrity of the system"*[19].

It should be noted that the negation of or resistance to capitalistic form of development does not mean the blind negation of all the technical advancement or scientific achievements, rather the critique is that, new technology, which no one dismisses, the key vehicle behind contemporary globalisation has been treated in a specialised fashion separated from the changing national and international context. The theory and the practice of new technology-the unique nature of innovations, production capacity, and diffusion and development-have, thus to be revamped[20].

d. The Myths of Productivity and Unproductivity

The main argument used for the industrialisation of food and corporatisation of agriculture is the low productivity of the small farmer. For many, biotechnology and genetic engineering will seal this gap and it is pointed out that "few newly developed technologies have occasioned as much optimism as biotechnology"[21]. According to those

---

[18] N.S.Jodha, *Sustainable Development in Fragile Environments* (Ahmedabad: Centre for Environment Education, 1995), 14.

[19] *Ibid.*

[20] Sumit Roy, *Globalisation, ICT and Developing Nations* (New Delhi: Sage Publications, 2005,), 20.

[21] Henk Hobbelink, "Biotechnology and the Future of Agriculture", in Vandana Shiva & Ingunn Moser (eds), *Biopolitics: A Feminist and Ecological Reader on Biotechnology* (London: Zed Books, 1995), 226.

supporters, yields per hectare will be doubled or tripled, super plants that produce their own fertiliser and pesticides will be developed, and new useful products will be derived from the same crops. Often it is stressed as a particular advantage of the technology that will improve food security for small farmers in the Third World, because of its potential to reduce the need for expensive inputs and its capability to adapt crops to the marginal soils on which small farmers often have to work[22]. However the introduction of high production varieties led to the gradual neglect of cultivars and local varieties which were remarkably sturdy and adaptable to their growing conditions[23]. Agricultural policies of the W.T.O are categorised according to whether they have a significant effect on production and they are[24]:

- Policies that do have a substantial impact on the patterns and flow of trade are classified as the "amber box"

- Policies that are not deemed to have a major effort on production and trade are classified as the "green box",

- Policies that fall in between are called the "blue box".

Quantitative production is the 'mantra' that is envisioned through globalisation to enhance 'growth'. Food Security has been replaced by the concept of Productivity. When food security was made external to food production, an illusion of growth was created. However the argument of

---

[22] Henk Hobbelink, "Biotechnology and the Future of Agriculture"... 226.

[23] Robert Ali Brac De La Perriere & Franck Seuret (eds), *Brave New Seeds: The Threat of GM Crops To Farmers* (London: Zed Books, 2000), 14.

[24] Vandana Shiva, *Globalisation of Agriculture* (New Delhi: Research Foundation for Science, Technology and Ecology, 2000), 6.

increased food availability through industrial breeding and centralised production based on intensive chemical inputs is flawed on five counts. Vandana Shiva states them as follows[25]:

- Industrial breeding focuses on partial yields of single crops rather than total system yields of multiple crops and integrated systems.

- Industrial breeding focuses on yields of one or two globally traded commodities, not on the diverse crops that people eat. Industrial breeding focuses on quantity per acre rather than nutrition per acre. In fact, nutrition per acre has come down as a result of industrial agriculture.

- Industrial breeding uses natural resources intensively and wastefully. If productivity is defined on the bases of resource use, industrial agriculture has very low productivity and it undermines food security by using up resources that could have been directly used, if not wasted in a non-sustainable system of production, to produce more food.

- Centralised food systems measure traded food, and do not measure the disappearance of locally consumed and foods hoarded at household and community level. This leads to national food security being built by undermining local food security.

- Ecological alternatives can increase food supply through biodiversity intensification instead of chemical intensification and through strengthening local food security.

---

[25] Vandana Shiva, "The Green Revolution and After", Books for Change, *The Great Grain Drain* (Bangalore: Books for Change, 1998), 18.

Vandana Shiva dismisses the claims of large farms being productive and small farmers being unproductive and asserts the other way round taking into account the diversity of yields. For her, as Dr. Bandopadhyay pointed out, even the World Development Report (WDR) has accepted that small farms are more productive than large ones[26]. Many examples are cited in this regard. In Brazil, the productivity of a 0-10ha farm was $85/ha while the productivity of a 500ha farm was $2/ha. In India, a 0-5 acre farm had a productivity of ₹ 735/acre while a 35 acre farm had a productivity of ₹ 346/acre[27]. Even biologically, small diverse farms have higher productivity than large monoculture farms as long as multiple yields are taken into account[28]. According to Vandana Shiva, *Productivity of monocultures is low in the context of diverse outputs and needs. It is high only in the restricted context of output of 'part of a part' of the forest and farm biomass; e.g. 'High yield" plantations pick one tree species among thousands; of yields of one part of the tree (e.g. pulp wood). Similarly high yield green revolution cropping patterns pick one crop among hundred, e.g. wheat for yields of one part of the wheat plant (only grain). These high partial yields do not translate into high total yields. Productivity is therefore different depending on whether it is measured in a framework of diversity or uniformity. Biodiversity based productivity measures show that small farmers can feed the world because in terms of multiple yields they have high productivity[29].* Moreover productivity in traditional farming practices has always

---

[26] Vandana Shiva, Globalisation of Agriculture and the Growth of Food Insecurity (New Delhi: Research Foundation for Science, Technology and Natural Resource Policy, 1996), 16.

[27] *Ibid.*, 17.

[28] *Ibid.*

[29] *Ibid.*

been high if it is remembered that very little external inputs are required[30].

e. The Myths of Efficiency and Inefficiency

On the logic of comparative advantage it is argued that a nation can enhance efficiency in resource use and hence net welfare, by producing and exporting commodities in which it is relatively efficient, and importing commodities in which it is relatively not so[31]. For Vandana Shiva, however, "The category of "efficiency" depends on the context in which it is measured[32]. Financially efficient systems can be ecologically very inefficient, and efficiency with respect to labour inputs is totally different from efficiency with respect to capital inputs[33]. In free trade, it is not countries but corporations which export and import and what is "efficient" for corporations need not be "efficient" for the countries in which they operate"[34].

f. Ownership of Resources

People like Jakhanwala[35] insist that 'we cannot produce more through increased equity and support that more food be produced in any mode to alleviate poverty'. Hence he justifies the transfer of resources from small holders to corporations and industrialists on grounds that 'higher production needs inequity because larger farmers are more efficient'[36]. Nevertheless, the threat of a totally controlled

---

[30] *Op.cit*, 30.

[31] Vandana Shiva, *Globalisation of Agriculture and the Growth of Food Insecurity*,...4.

[32] *Ibid.*, 5.

[33] *Ibid.*

[34] *Ibid.*

[35] He was the Secretary, Ministry of Food and Civil Supplies of the Indian Government.

[36] Vandana Shiva, Globalisation of Agriculture and the Growth of Food Insecurity,...16.

agriculture, with farmers reduced to the rank of mere sowers of seeds developed in laboratories by multinationals, looms large. With transgenic plants, the freedom of agricultural practice and liberty of choice is reduced as the farmer works with a patented product which is subject to very specific conditions of use[37]. Patent protection implies the exclusion of farmers' right over the resources. This will undermine the very foundations of agriculture. In addition, there is the inevitable disappearance of knowledge as farmers lose their traditional role as guardians of biodiversity and breeders-adapters of environmentally advantaged varieties[38]. Biodiversity, land and water are the three vital resources that the majority of our people depend on for their livelihood and survival. Intellectual property rights are taking away the living resources and biodiversity from the people and converting them into corporate monopolies. Seeds, medicinal plants and neem plant-based pesticides, which have been the basis of people's livelihood in agriculture and health care, are being appropriated through new patent regimes enforced through GATT[39].

g. Concentration of Ownership

The transfer of ownership from small holdings to larger corporations is based on the assumption that productivity is less in small farms. Thus the agriculture ministry states: "Limited land holding per capita in India is a great obstacle which inhibits large scale mechanisation and adopting

---

[37] Robert Ali Brac De La Perriere & Franck Seuret (eds), *Brave New Seeds: The Threat of GM Crops To Farmers,...* 16.

[38] *Op.cit,* 16.

[39] Vandana Shiva, "Democracy in the Age of Globalisation", in Ajit Muricken, ed., *Globalisation and SAP: Trends &Impact- An Overview* (Mumbai: Vikas Adhyayan Kendra, 1997), 68.

other measures for increasing the productivity and bringing down the unit cost of production"[40]. Similarly, an analysis of Removal of Import Restrictions states, *"If we want our agriculture to become competitive with rest of the world we must go for modernisation of this sector with improved technology. This would require huge private investments; but, a large proportion of our farmers in bottom category are resource poor and cannot afford this. The very size of such farms discourages mechanisation and use of modern equipments which are essential to increase efficiency. The time has come when something has to be done to put a floor on the bottom side of holding"[41]*. This mode of capitalistic agriculture development under globalisation, which concentrated on production and productivity, increased the concentration of land ownership, thus leading to the marginalisation of the small farmers. However the arguments for small farms are that they can, in the right circumstances, be more productive and efficient than large ones without the hidden costs and can more easily undertake environmentally friendly and low-risk practices. Trade liberalisation policies are leading to the alienation of natural resources like land, water and biodiversity from peasant communities and the concentration of their ownership.

h. Nation State as Against Global Monopolies

Globalisation does mean 'less government' for regulation of business and commerce. This doesn't imply a transfer of power from the state apparatus to the people rather consolidation and less responsible power into the hands of global corporations. Moreover, in the 'developing' world, neo-liberal hegemonic globalisation relegates economic

---

[40] Vandana Shiva, *Globalisation of Agriculture Food Security and Sustainability* ... 38.

[41] *Ibid.,* 38.

growth to market mechanisms and so de-politicises development. It relocates eco-political decisions away from the national state to multilateral institutions and multinational corporations and so undermines national governments[42]. The overall effect was inevitably to devitalise national and especially local political institutions. However, as D.L.Sheth emphasises, "an important, if unanticipated, consequence of the decline of institutional politics was the revitalisation of old social movements"[43]. For "based on such an assessment of globalisation's adverse impact both for development and democracy, grass roots movements conceive their politics in the direction of achieving two inter-related goals: a)re-politicising development and b)reinventing participatory democracy"[44].

i. Decentralisation of Resources

The major democratic issue emerging in India is the right to survival of the large number of poor people who derive their livelihood from natural resources-land, water and biodiversity. Along with the privatisation trend is the trend towards concentration. As Hobbelink has put it, 'the few are becoming fewer and the big grow bigger'[45]. People's movements are demanding that power should not be concentrated in institutions of the centralised nation-states but should be distributed throughout society and should be dispersed through a multiplicity of institutions, with more power at the local level, controlled by local

---

[42] Rudolf C Heredia, "Inclusive Development, Liberating Modernity: India Civilization at the Crossroads.1", Vidyajyoti Journal of Theological Reflection, Vol.71,Jan-Dec. 2007, 39.

[43] *Ibid.*

[44] *Ibid.*

[45] Quoted by Vandana Shiva, *Monocultures of the Mind* (Dehradun: Natraj Publishers, 1993), 119.

communities and their institutions[46]. The on-going struggles all over the places concerning agriculture, land, water and nature, on the one hand are struggles for the right of life, and on the other are the struggles for the right to ownership (property). The struggles for the right to life are said to be basic and much higher than the struggle for the right to ownership. The right to ownership places emphasis more on individualism whereas the right to life places emphasis more on community. Right to life builds within the people a sense of their humanity and their links to earth, its resources and natural process which sustains all life, and give sense of alienation from land, alienation from community and nature. The right to ownership gives the sense of economy while the right to life gives the sense of ecology and economy.

j. Growth from Below

Globalisation from above is a hegemonic exploitation, whereas a globalisation from below could be a liberating movement[47]. What we should envision is a process that can overturn the whole ongoing process. Communities, Groups and Nationalities are dictated by the international agencies that promote hegemony of culture and economic exploitation. What is absent is a participatory mode of development paradigm that includes the aspirations of local communities and the people at the periphery. Wide varieties of local knowledge and experience could be a potential source to the sustainable growth and mutuality between human and non-human life.

---

[46] Vandana Shiva, "Democracy in the Age of Globalisation", in Ajit Muricken, ed., *Globalisation and SAP: Trends & Impact- An Overview* (Mumbai: Vikas Adhyayan Kendra, 1997), 72.

[47] Rudolf C Heredia, "Inclusive Development, Liberating Modernity: India Civilization at the Crossroads.1", Vidyajyoti Journal of Theological Reflection, Vol.71, Jan-Dec. 2007, 36.

k. *Monoculture Vs Biodiversity*

Biological diversity refers to all living organisms, their genetic material and the ecosystems of which they are a part. It is usually described at three levels: genetic, species, and ecosystem diversity[48].

Genetic diversity is the variation of genes between and within species. Genetic diversity within a species permits it to adapt to new pests and diseases, and to changes in environment, climate and agricultural methods. Biological diversity is the cornerstone of sustainable agriculture and world food security. For many farming communities, diversity- be it social, cultural, economic or genetic- means security. Genetic diversity provides security for the farmer against pests, disease, and unexpected climatic conditions. It also helps small-scale farmers to maximise production in the highly variable, and often marginal or stressed environments in which they tend to cultivate their crops, herd or livestock and fish.

Traditionally, small-scale farmers not only use a wide range of crop species in their complex farming systems of intercropping, polyculture and agro forestry, but also use several varieties within each crop[49]. It is this biological diversity that forms the basis of their production systems, and their food security. "Diversity, like music or a dialect, is part of the community that produced it. It cannot exist for long without that community and the circumstances that give rise to it"[50]. "Only in use can diversity continue to evolve and no freezing technology can relieve us of the

---

[48] *www.rafi.org,* downloaded on 05.02.2007.

[49] Henk Hobbelink, "Biotechnology and the Future of Agriculture", in Vandana Shiva & Ingunn Moser (eds), *Biopolitics: A Feminist and Ecological Reader on Biotechnology* (London: Zed Books, 1995), 232.

[50] Quoted by Bas Wielenga, *Towards an Eco-Just Society* (Bangalore: Centre for Social Action, 1999), 70.

responsibility to preserve agricultural diversity for ourselves and all future generations"[51].

According to Vandana Shiva, the crucial characteristic of monocultures is that they do not merely displace alternatives, they destroy their own basis[52]. They are neither tolerant of other systems, nor are they able to reproduce themselves sustainably[53]. Vandana Shiva opines that the monoculture paradigm of the Green revolution and industrial agriculture focuses on single functions of single species, and fails to take yields of diverse species and diverse functions into account and hence not sustainable[54]. Globally, the biotechnology solution imposes an increased dependence on inputs. This tendency increases intensive monoculture and steadily marginalises small-scale farmers who are already the most vulnerable to hunger[55]. Moreover biodiversity based productivity measures show that small farmers can feed the world because in terms of multiple yields they have high productivity[56]. It is also argued that, *through all the years of the Green Revolution, biodiversity was baffled in several ways. Firstly, the diversity of local cropping systems was partially swept away by the spread of monoculture. Then, the range of cultivated species shrank while rice and wheat gained ground both in irrigated farming and in rain fed systems. Finally, the range of cultivate varieties within a single species*

---

[51] *Ibid.*

[52] Vandana Shiva, *Monocultures of the Mind* (Dehradun: Natraj Publishers, 1993), 50.

[53] *Ibid.*

[54] Vandana Shiva, *Betting On Biodiversity* (New Delhi: Research Foundation for Science, Technology and Ecology, 2006), 1.

[55] Robert Ali Brac De La Perriere & Franck Seuret (eds), *Brave New Seeds: The Threat of GM Crops To Farmers* (London: Zed Books, 2000), 13.

[56] Vandana Shiva, *Globalisation of Agriculture and the Growth of Food Insecurity...* 17.

has been declining since the sixties[57]. Vandana Shiva opines that biodiversity cannot be conserved until diversity is made the logic of production and if production continues to be based on the logic of uniformity and homogenisation, uniformity will continue to displace diversity[58]. Thus for her, uniformity as a pattern of production becomes inevitable only in a context of control and profitability.

l. Food Security

The concept of food security is interpreted in a variety of ways. However, physical and economic access to food at the household level at all times to ensure healthy and active life is the crux of food security[59]. Food security necessarily results from the interplay of three determining factors: food production, food availability and access to food. Food security is thus related not only to the physical availability of food but also to the accessibility,i.e.ability to buy food, which is related to remunerative employment, which in turn, is linked with the access to land and employment opportunities in agriculture and agro-based activities[60]. Hence food security is a human rights issue. According to Vandana Shiva, it includes the right to resources, the right to work, the right to cultural diversity, the right to health and the right to information[61]. Nevertheless the WTO approach to agriculture and food

---

[57] Robert Ali Brac De La Perriere & Franck Seuret (eds), *Brave New Seeds: The Threat of GM Crops To Farmers*, ...45.

[58] Vandana Shiva, *Monocultures of the Mind* (Dehradun: Natraj Publishers, 1993), 146.

[59] V.P.Ragahavan, "Agricultural Trade Policy and Food Security in India: Issues and Challenges", in *Social Action*, (New Delhi: A Social Action Trust Publication, January-March, Vol: 56, No.1) 2.

[60] *Ibid.*

[61] Vandana Shiva, *Globalisation of Agriculture and the Growth of Food Insecurity* (New Delhi: Research Foundation for Science, Technology and Natural Resource Policy, 1996), 3.

security is trade linked and described as 'food security by way of trade'. This implies that the quest for self-sufficiency is no longer necessary rather would be met by trade imports in a largely liberalised world. According to Vandana Shiva, 'Food security is neither dollars in the pockets, nor food in the elevators of Cargill rather lies in ecologically resilient and economically efficient farming systems which provide livelihoods to farmers and self-sufficiency in food at the household, community, regional and national levels, while providing safe and nutritious food to consumers[62]. On the other hand it is repeatedly argued that food security does not depend on food "self sufficiency" (growing your own food as a country) but on food "self reliance" (buying your food from international markets)[63]. In her welcome address on globalisation and Food, Dr. Vandna Shiva said, "The US and other industrialised countries of the North are trying to change the meaning of food security from being a fundamental human right to participation in global markets, which excludes the large number of poor without adequate purchasing power"[64]. Increasing productivity to feed the needy is the core theme of genetic engineering enclosed in globalisation. However analysis shows that poverty is escalating. If poverty is defined in terms of a minimum consumption of 2400 calories per capita per day in rural areas, then based on this criterion, 75 per cent of the rural population in India today is poor, compared with 56 per cent in 1973-74[65]. This is because

---

[62] *Ibid.,* 12

[63] *Ibid.,* 14.

[64] *Op.cit,* 4.

[65] Rudolf C Heredia, "Inclusive Development, Liberating Modernity: India Civilization at the Crossroads.1", Vidyajyoti Journal of Theological Reflection, Vol.71, Jan-Dec. 2007, 32.

structural adjustment policies did not, on the whole, take food security into consideration. In many countries like India they led to the sudden end of state support for agriculture and falls in food production. Inequality and poverty in Indian have therefore been exacerbated by liberalisation and globalisation.

3. Methods Employed in Promoting Sustainable Growth

Participatory appropriate technology development ensures the justice that people are able to incorporate their values and knowledge in the technology they use. Farmer's knowledge and value systems are inevitable in promoting sustainable growth. It dismantles the inequitable domination of Western forms of knowledge over the lives of millions of people. Traditional forms of knowledge are pertinent in countering the manipulative agenda of the reductionistic science and technological approach. According to Nicanor Perlas, if the following changes are brought about, they will make other subsequent changes much easier and faster[66]. Vandana Shiva too proposes identical solutions to a culture-specific, farmer-specific, food security enabling, sustainable mode of agriculture.

1. A culture specific agrarian reform programme.

2. Non-token participation of all affected parties in the policy areas affecting agriculture

3. Reform of the national research network so as to make it more responsive to the needs of sustainable agriculture.

4. Stricter implementation of environment; and pesticide regulatory laws.

---

[66] Nicanor Perlas, "The Seven Dimensions of Sustainable Agriculture", in Vandana Shiva & Ingunn Moser (eds), *Biopolitics: A Feminist and Ecological Reader on Biotechnology* (London: Zed Books, 1995), 261.

5. A redirection of government support away from the production of export crops towards meeting basic food security needs.

6. Strengthening of peoples' initiatives in all areas of agriculture.

7. NGO and farmer participation in the regulation of pesticides.

8. Greater incentives for the production of organic fertilisers, on-farm or off-farm, the latter being a transitional stage

9. Redirection of credit policies so that pesticides are decoupled from credit packages and credit support for sustainable agriculture is increased.

Vandana Shiva brings in comparison three models of agriculture to evaluate the methods:

Three Models of Agriculture[67]

	The Green Revolution	The Corporate Model	The Sustainable, Farmer Centered Model
Driving Force	Multilateral agencies and government driven	Corporations trade driven	Small farmer led, nature and human need driven
Structure of Production & Distribution	Centralised/ long distance, high "food miles"	More Centralised, longer distances, "food miles".	Decentralised, local and regional transport, low 'food miles'

---

[67] Vandana Shiva, *Globalisation of Agriculture and the Growth of Food Insecurity* (New Delhi: Research Foundation for Science, Technology and Natural Resource Policy, 1996), 24.

	The Green	The Corporate	The Sustainable
Preferred *Methods*	Chemical/ High External Inputs	Higher external inputs/increased chemicalisation/ genetic engineering.	Organic/ Ecological/Low external Inputs
Status of *Diversity*	Monoculture	More Extensive Monocultures	Polycultures
Productivity	Low resource use producti- vity, high environmental subsidies.	Lower resource use productivity, higher environ- mental subsidies	High resource use productivity, no environmental subsidies.
Socio-Ecological *Characteristics*	Non sustainable/ Undemocratic	Non-democratic/ Non sustainable	Democratic/ Sustainable

a. Land Reforms

Land reforms are inevitable in the process towards a sustainable growth. Nevertheless, land reform laws which had attempted to undo concentration of land ownership under zamindari are themselves being undone. One of the major targets of the World Bank agricultural reforms is the abrogation of land ceiling laws[68]. On the other hand, the fact is that the state of Bengal was showing the highest rate of growth of 6.5% for agriculture as a result of land reform, while the rate of growth for India was a mere 3%[69]. Redistributive land reforms-dividing large farms into

---

[68] Vandana Shiva, "Democracy in the Age of Globalisation", in Ajit Muricken, ed., *Globalisation and SAP: Trends and Impact- An Overview* (Mumbai: Vikas Adhyayan Kendra, 1997), 70.

[69] Vandana Shiva, *Globalisation of Agriculture and the Growth of Food Insecurity* (New Delhi: Research Foundation for Science, Technology and Natural Resource Policy, 1996), 17.

smaller units has led to more food per hectare in a number of developing countries[70]. When, for example, land in the Piaui district of northeast Brazil was redistributed to small farmers it spurred a new interest among farmers and the yields increased by between 10 and 40 per cent; and on irrigated fields, between 30 to 70 percent[71]. In China, the shift from large farms to small holdings has witnessed an unprecedented rise in farm output, enabling millions to escape from poverty[72]. Land security for poor can therefore lead to food security[73].

b. Traditional Farming Systems

Traditional farming systems are based on mixed and rotational cropping systems of cereals, pulses, oilseeds with diverse varieties of each crop[74]. One of the most impressive gains found by the Essex University study was achieved by small farmers in Madagascar. After they employed a new way of growing rice, yields of around two tonnes per hectare shot up to around 8 to 10 tonnes per hectare without chemical fertilisers, pesticides or expensive seed varieties[75]. The method they employed was simple; "Traditionally, rice is transplanted into fields at around eight weeks, but with SRI[76], seedlings are transplanted at around six days and planted individually, enabling farmers to useless seed. Using their own seed, some 20,000 farmers have now adopted the method in Madagascar and the

---

[70] John Madeley, *Food for All: Can Hunger be Halved?* (London: The Panos Institute, 2001), 22.

[71] *Ibid.*

[72] *Ibid.,* 23.

[73] *Ibid.*

[74] Vandana Shiva, *Monocultures of the Mind* (Dehradun: Natraj Publishers, 1993), 40.

[75] John Madeley, *Food for All: Can Hunger be Halved?* ... 25.

[76] System of Rice Intensification.

yields have proved sustainable[77]. Vandana Shiva, in her analysis states that, "Productivity in traditional farming practices has always been high if it is remembered that very little external inputs are required"[78]. Traditional agriculture has also controlled the problem of pests through crop rotation and the use of different crops in different reasons[79]. The people did not use pesticides and they did not recognise the concept of 'weeds', as they knew how to utilise everything for different purposes[80].

c. Local Resource Focus

If agriculture has to meet the increasing demands, means have to be found to counter erosion and alienation. Experiences in the wasteland development programme indicate that this will be possible only if local people get control over local resources and have a stake in the increase of biomass production, while using organic farming methods to increase soil fertility and augment water supply- for all- through watershed management[81]. Other measures should include appropriate water management policies, reduction of subsidies that encourage wasteful use of inputs, better definition of ownership and user rights to resources including land[82]. Moreover decentralisation of resources can bring vibrancy, vitality and relevance to farmers and can provide a democratic alternative to the monopoly forces of globalisation. Local

---

[77] John Madeley, *Food for All: Can Hunger be Halved?* ...25.

[78] Vandana Shiva, *Betting On Biodiversity* (New Delhi: Research Foundation for Science, Technology and Ecology, 2006), 9.

[79] Bas Wielenga, *Towards an Eco-Just Society* (Bangalore: Centre for Social Action, 1999), 30.

[80] *Ibid.*

[81] *Ibid.*, 34.

[82] Yoginder Alagh, Foreword in *The Great Grain Drain* (Bangalore: Books for Change, 1998), x.

knowledge systems are a rich resource contributive to sustainability. For Vandana Shiva, however, modern agriculture focuses exclusively on agricultural commodity production. It displaces local knowledge systems which view agriculture as the production of diverse food crops with internal inputs, and replaces it with monocultures of introduced varieties needing external inputs[83]. Alternate land use systems, namely agro-forestry, agri-horticulture, silvi-pastoral and silvi-horticulture can be profitably be adopted in both arable and non arable lands as these systems offer conservation of soil resources and a stable production means in a rain fed system[84].

d. External Inputs Vs Internal Inputs

Agricultural intensification was the strategy chosen to promote agricultural development and food security. This applied both to food crops and to high value cash crops such as vegetables and fruit in mountains and oilseeds in the dry areas. Agricultural intensification had two key dimensions. First, it led to a narrowed focus of programmes, both in terms of choice of priority corps as well as their emphasised attributes (e.g. growth of grain yield rather than optimisation of total biomass). Second, it meant high input-intensive cropping, with the emphasis on increased application of high cost external inputs. Apart from making farmers dependent on high cost external inputs, agricultural intensification led to the loss of agro-biodiversity and the marginalisation of several local crops and crop varieties[85]. It is noted that in several valleys

---

[83] Vandana Shiva, *Monocultures of the Mind* (Dehradun: Natraj Publishers, 1993), 59.

[84] G.K.Veeresh, ed., *Organic farming for Alleviation of Rural Poverty* (Bangalore: Association for Promotion of Organic Farming, 2006), 13.

[85] N.S.Jodha, *Sustainable Development in Fragile Environments* (Ahmedabad: Centre for Environment Education, 1995), 80.

of the middle mountains of Nepal and the U.P. hills in India, there used to be more than a dozen types of rice; however at present, in most of the rice growing areas, one finds hardly two or three varieties in use, developed by the agricultural research centers. *High input-intensive cropping, and the choice of technologies that facilitate it, are an unavoidable consequence of the exclusive focus on yield levels. Both for multiple cropping and for high yields of individual crops, the dependence on external (chemical) inputs have rapidly increased. This is partly due to the very design of the technologies employed, and partly to the inability of the local resource regenerative systems (such as nutrient-recycling through farming-forestry linkages, or biological control of diseases and pests through specific crop rotations) to meet high and temporally concentrated demands of the new systems.*[86] For Vandana Shiva, external inputs such as pesticides, herbicides and chemical fertilisers destroy agricultural biodiversity through their ecological impacts. Vandana Shiva thus advocates that sustainability requires a shift from external inputs to low-external input or internal input-agriculture[87]. She opines that the supply of internal inputs can only be based on the regeneration of agricultural biodiversity. Internal inputs that are substitutes for external input include green manure species and species used for pest control as well as livestock and farming systems that produce fodder for livestock[88]. While external inputs are part of a strategy for chemical intensification of agriculture, internal inputs are part of a strategy for the biodiversity[89].

---

[86] *Ibid.*, 81.

[87] Vandana Shiva, 'The Green Revolution and After', in *The Great Grain Drain* (Bangalore: Books for Change, 1998), 29.

[88] *Ibid.*

[89] *Ibid.*

e. Polyculture as Against Monoculture

According to Vandana Shiva, in a polyculture system, five units of input are used to produce 100 units of food thus having a productivity of 20 while in an industrial monoculture, 300 units of input are used to produce 100 units of food, thus having a productivity of .33[90]. The 295 units of wasted inputs could have provided 5900 units of food and thus the industrial system leads to a decline of 5900 units of food[91]. For Vandana Shiva, the polyculture system which has been called 'low yielding' and hence incapable of meeting food needs is therefore sixty times more productive than the so called 'high yielding monoculture'[92].

f. Local Food Security and Local Markets

According to Vandana Shiva, the impact of the new agriculture policy has been to promote a shift from food grains to vegetables and perishable commodities[93]. While grains can be stored and consumed locally, potatoes and tomatoes must be sold immediately. A vegetable centered policy thus decreases food security and increases farmers vulnerability to the market. While this promotes monocultures of perishable commodities, local food security cannot be ensured. In the 'Peoples' Charter for Food Security'[94], it is stated that "we believe that there is

---

[90] Vandana Shiva, *Globalisation of Agriculture and the Growth of Food Insecurity* (New Delhi: Research Foundation for Science, Technology and Natural Resource Policy, 1996), 17.

[91] Vandana Shiva, 'The Green Revolution and After', in *The Great Grain Drain* (Bangalore: Books for Change, 1998), 23.

[92] Vandana Shiva, *Globalisation of Agriculture and the Growth of Food Insecurity,...* 17.

[93] *www.zmarg.org*, downloaded on 31.01.2007.

[94] The Peoples' Charter for Food Security was evolved by the coalition of Peoples' Organizations, NGO's, Trade Unions, and other concerned people

need for greater local self-sufficiency in regard to food production, in accordance with local consumption practices and priorities".[95]

g. Organic Farming

Organic farming is one approach to sustainable agriculture. Organic farming is being recognised as necessary for environmental protection, health protection and the protection of food security. Organic Farming is a production system that avoids or largely excludes the use of synthetically produced fertilisers, pesticides, growth regulators, and livestock feed additives. Sustainable agriculture means not only the withdrawal of three things-synthetic chemicals, hybrid-genetically modified seeds and heavy agricultural implements; it is an elaborate system that tries to simulate the conditions found in nature[96]. It is also multiculture, intercropping, use of farmyard manure and remnants, mulching and application of integrated pest management[97]. As far as possible, organic farming relies on crop rotations, crop residues, animal manures, legumes, green manures, off-farm organic wastes, and aspects of biological pest control to maintain soil productivity and tillage, to supply plant nutrients, and to control insects, weeds, and other pests. Also, in organic farming, attempts are made to replace the market

---

including environmentalists, legal experts, economists, nutrition and food security experts, journalists etc. at the two day Policy Dialogue on Trade Liberalization and Food security; organized by the Research Foundation for Science, technology and Natural Resource Policy and Third World Network (India) on 4-5 February 1995 at National Co-operative Union of India, New Delhi-110 016.

[95] Vandana Shiva, *Globalisation of Agriculture and the Growth of Food Insecurity,...* 27.

[96] *www.hinduonnet.com,* downloaded on 31.01.2007.

[97] *www.hinduonnet.com,* downloaded on 31.01.2007.

dependent inorganic nutrient supplying inputs with on farm generated, hence self reliant bio-mass resources and processes to the extent possible[98]. In developing countries, organic agriculture, usually in the form of intercropping, has been the norm for centuries. In recent years there has been an enforced return to organic farming as farmers have been unable to afford the chemical needed for intensive agriculture. One of the features of organic farming is that it can be done in any situation from lowest rainfall areas to highest rainfall areas. Organic principals are location specific for improving the productivity[99]. Managing local natural resources like seeds, manure, plant protection technique, rain water harvesting will reduce the input cost and improve farm income. Organic farming as a method exists to develop, and promote sustainable relationships between the soil, plants, animals, people, and the biosphere, in order to produce healthy food and other products while protecting and enhancing the environment. A major figure in the movement to enhance such a position is noted German writer and economist Ernst.F.Schumacher who encapsulated much of the thinking behind a return to the soil in the book *Small is Beautiful: Economics as if People Mattered,* published in 1973. Vandana Shiva, in her writings as well as in her own agricultural farm in Dehradun follows organic farming methods.

Vandana Shiva reiterates the traditional forms of agricultural methods as being sustainable. For Vandana Shiva, all systems of sustainable agriculture, whether of the past or the future, work on the basis of the perennial

---

[98] G.K.Veeresh, ed., *Organic farming for Alleviation of Rural Poverty* (Bangalore: Association for Promotion of Organic Farming, 2006), 7.

[99] *Ibid.,* 4.

principles of diversity and reciprocity[100]. These two principles are interrelated. In her opinion, diversity gives rise to the ecological space for give and take, for mutuality and reciprocity[101]. According to Vandana Shiva, destruction of diversity is linked to the creation of monocultures, and with the creation of monocultures, the self-regulation and decentred organisation of diverse systems gives way to external inputs and external centralised control[102]. For her, closely linked to the issue of diversity and uniformity is the issue of productivity. Higher yields and higher production have been the main push for the introduction of uniformity and the logic of the assembly line. She opines that, the imperative of growth generates the imperative for monocultures yet this growth is, in large measure, a socially constructed, value-laden category[103]. For her, diversity as a pattern of production is not merely a concept of conservation rather one which ensures pluralism and decentralisation[104]. It challenges the dominant paradigm of 'control', homogeneity and development through 'trade' and re-affirms the concepts of decentralisation, diversity and mutuality of creation.

---

[100] Vandana Shiva, *Monocultures of the Mind* (Dehradun: Natraj Publishers, 1993), 147.

[101] *Ibid.*

[102] *Ibid.*

[103] *Ibid.*

[104] *Ibid.*

Chapter 4

ETHICAL EVALUATION AND CONCLUSION

1. Introduction

Agriculture is a way of life, a tradition, which for centuries, has shaped the thought, the outlook, the culture and the economic life of the people of India. Agriculture, therefore, is and will continue to be central to all strategies for planned socio-economic development of the country. Over 200 million Indian farmers and farm workers have been the backbone of India's agriculture. With more than two-thirds of our population still living in rural areas and surviving of agriculture, agricultural development cannot but be a core issue for 'progress' in India. Many envision an economic progress while others envisage a sustainable progress. It is also worth noting that India would need to produce additional food grains of 100 and 160 million tones by 2030 and 2050 AD respectively to feed its projected population[1]. Hence productivity does matter in the prevailing context. Nevertheless it is increasingly recognised that who produces food and where it is produced may actually be as or more important than how much is produced. There is also a severe threat to the natural processes that sustain the global ecosphere and life on earth due to various factors including declining

---

[1] S.A.Patil and H.B.Babalad, "Organic farming and Sustainable Agriculture-Key Issues", in G.K.Veeresh, ed., *Organic Inputs for Organic Farming* (Bangalore: Association for Promotion of Organic Farming, 2002), 7.

natural resources and environmental degradation. This is the context which necessitates an evaluation of the present scenario in the agriculture sector that is lifeline to a majority population of India.

a. Towards Evolving a Framework to Evaluate Agriculture Globalisation

The question of 'development' guaranteed through globalisation and trade becomes the focal point in evaluating agriculture globalisation. 'Development' and 'Humanitarianism' are discerned by many from different perspectives and therefore acquired a wide range of meanings. Here the contention is to trace out the undergirding principles, which are inherent in these development and humanistic paradigms. Development in any way cannot be devoid of the participation of human beings. It must not only include human beings but also the creation as a whole. The possibility and need for a balanced relationship between humans and nature in agricultural civilisations is resought to sustain ecology and justice. *Core to the concept of sustainability is the need to preserve natural resources for everyone for all times.* The reality of declining resources, unlimited trade sponsored productivity, irresponsible consumption; injustice and the lack of a long-term perspective are all inclusive in the evaluation. In spite of being pursuing organic farming or any other traditional farming methods, it is a fact that, it is inevitable in agriculture to have some sort of control over nature in order to produce best results. Modernity is not kept out of the agriculture sector to keep it safe, rather farmers with their immense experiences through generations have devised many attempts to modernise it. Nevertheless, in these attempts, the interference with nature has been kept within limits, as it is a matter of aiding nature or intensifying its processes. However, this contrasts with the violent interventions of external inputs, large-scale, production-oriented, market-oriented ideology ensued through the process of globalisation of agriculture. Market and profit oriented outlook and intense chemicalisation of agriculture and the interventions of genetic manipulation, have indisputably turned modern agriculture into an environmentally destructive occupation. Moreover, in periods of rapid technological transformation, it is assumed that society and people must adjust to change instead of technological change adjusting to the social values of equity, sustainability and participation[2]. This ideology is contested in the light of largely declining natural resources and imbalances in ecology. Globalisation of agriculture and its related paraphernalia is toeing an ideology which emphasises trade, better productivity through technology and progress. However in this process, the concept of diversity- which is inevitable to sustainability, food security and protection of natural resources is largely evaded. Sustainability of agriculture requires an alternative to the external intensification and external liberalisation of agriculture. Internal intensification which is based on biodiversity intensification will free agriculture communities from external dependence for purchase of seeds, agrichemicals and seeds. This will ensure a democratic space and security to the local communities dependent on agriculture. To be economical, accessible to all (development in its political essence) and to be sustainable, agriculture has to be ecologically diverse.

---

[2] Vandana Shiva, "Biotechnological Development and the Conservation of Biodiversity", in Vandana Shiva, Ingunn Moser, eds., *Biopolitics-A Feminist and Ecological Reader in Biotechnology* (London: Zed Books Ltd, 1995), 193.

b. E.F. Schumacher's[3] Development Paradigm

E.F.Schumacher basically unravels the maddened economic interest of human being which is unleashed on nature and thereby turning the habitat into a non-living and unsustainable one. He repudiates the cultural mindset of the industrialised and the urbanised that are on a spree to accumulate. According to Schumacher, the idolatry of economism largely contributes to the disregard of human values and reiterates violence, alienation and environmental destruction. For him, the industrialisation and depersonalisation of agriculture which leads to concentration, specialisation as well as negating labour for the sake of maximising profits will ultimately end up in the wider human habitat being standardised to dreariness. According to Schumacher, greed and envy demand continuous and limitless economic growth of a material kind, without proper regard for conservation, and this type of growth cannot possibly fit into a finite environment[4]. For Schumacher, "modern man does not experience himself as a part of nature but as an outside force destined to dominate and conquer it"[5]. The urge is to minimise the destruction caused to nature and creation

---

[3] E.F.Schumacher has been a Rhodes Scholar in economics, an economic advisor to the British Control Commission in postwar Germany, and for the twenty years prior to 1971, the top economist and head of planning at the British Coal Board. He was the president of the Soil Association, one of Britain's oldest organic farming organizations; founder and chairman of the Intermediate Technology Development Group, which specializes in tailoring tools, small-scale machines, and methods of production to the needs of developing countries; a sponsor of the Fourth World Movement, a British based campaign for political decentralization and regionalism; a director of the Scott Bader Company, a pioneering effort at common ownership and workers' control; a close student of Gandhi, non-violence and ecology.

[4] E.F.Schumacher, *Small is Beautiful: Economics as if People Mattered* (New York: Harper &Row Publishers, 1975), 263.

[5] *Ibid.*, 4.

as a whole; not by negligence but by an intimidating approach to garner wealth at all costs. Hence Schumacher states[6]:

> From an economic point of view, the central concept of wisdom is permanence. We must study the economics of permanence. Nothing makes economic sense unless its continuance for a long time can be projected without running into absurdities. There can be 'growth' towards a limited objective, but there cannot be unlimited, generalised growth. It is more than likely, as Gandhi said, that "Earth provides enough to satisfy every man's need but not for every man's (sic) greed."

Moreover Schumacher reiterates that the economics of permanence implies a profound reorientation of science and technology. For him, we need methods and equipments which are 1) cheap enough so that they are accessible to virtually everyone, 2) suitable for small-scale application and 3) compatible with man's (sic) need for creativity[7]. Out of these three characteristics is born non-violence and a relationship of man to nature which guarantees permanence[8]. Schumacher offers a critique to the purely technology intensive, trade-oriented, large-scale agriculture production activities on the basis that human are not producers of primary resources rather mere converters of them.

c. 'Small is Beautiful'

E.F.Schumacher's economics as explicated in "Small is Beautiful" is not part of the dominant style. On the contrary, his deliberate intention is to subvert "economic science" by calling its very assumption into question, right

---

6. *Ibid.*, 33.
7. E.F.Schumacher, *op.cit.*, 34.
8. *Ibid.*

down to its psychological and metaphysical foundations. According to Schumacher, "Bigness is the nemesis of anarchism, whether the bigness is that of public or private bureaucracies, because from bigness comes impersonality, insensitivity and a lust to concentrate abstract power"[9]. For him, the "small is free, efficient, creative, enjoyable, enduring"[10]. Schumacher advocates small scale operations as well towards the sustainability of human and nature. Thus for him, small-scale operations, no matter how numerous, are always less likely to be harmful to the natural environment than large-scale ones, simply because their individual force is small in relation to the recuperative forces of nature[11]. Furthermore, according to Schumacher, the most prosperous countries of his times are small while bigger nations are poor[12].

d. Hegemony of the Rich Capitalist Countries– A Dangerous Trend

In spite of globalisation being helpful in certain ways to the global community, globalisation of agriculture has by and large benefited the developed countries and the global corporations. There are different standpoints regarding the ever-increasing dominance of rich capitalist nations, especially the U.S. "American Empire" is a term of approval and optimism for some, and disparagement and danger for others. Neo-conservatives celebrate the imperial exercise of U.S power, which is a modern version of Rudyard Kipling's 'white man's burden'[13]. For them it is

---

[9] *Ibid.,* 4.

[10] *Ibid.*

[11] *Ibid.,* 36.

[12] *Ibid.,* 64.

[13] Ninan Koshy, 'The Global Empire', *Peoples' Reporter,* Vol.19, Issue 15 (Aug: 10-25, 2006), 3.

a liberal force that undercuts tyranny, terrorism, military aggression and weapons proliferation[14]. Critics who identify an emerging global empire meanwhile worry about its corrosive effect on democracy, its implications for the rest of the world, especially the weaker nations, and the threat it poses to international institutions, many of which were initiated by the U.S. and secured U.S. national interests[15]. Moreover the terms attributed to rich countries such as the U.S. is sharper than ever and the shift in terminology from 'dominance' to 'hegemony' to 'empire' is significant, above all, because it highlights the classic concept of direct political control by an imperial centre. It is a question of indefinite dominance. The rhetoric, concept, strategy and policy of the empire camp are not new. The difference is that they are now in absolute power[16].

> Moreover, modern western knowledge is a particular cultural system with a particular relationship to power. It has, however, been projected as above and beyond culture and politics. Its relationship with the project of economic development has been invisible; and therefore it has become a more effective legitimiser for the homogenisation of the world and the erosion of its ecological and cultural richness. The power by which the dominant knowledge system has subjugated all others makes it exclusive and undemocratic. Democratising of knowledge becomes a central precondition for human liberation because the contemporary knowledge system excludes the humane by its very structure[17].

---

14 *Ibid.*

15 *Ibid.*

16 *Ibid.*

17 Vandana Shiva, *Monocultures of the Mind* (Dehradun: Natraj Publishers, 1993), 60.

The ruinous attitude and ideology of the rich developed nations is best described in Schumacher's words as follows;

...as for the developed countries from which the corrupting ethos of progress goes out: more and more their "growthmania" distorts their environments and robs the world of its nonrenewable resources for no better end than to increase the output of ballistic missiles, electric hairdryers, and eight-track stereophonic tape recorders....but in the statistics of the economic index such mad waste measures out as 'productivity', and all looks rosy[18]. The ideological position of the rich capitalists is derogatory to the development prospects of a majority around the world. The modern economy is propelled by a frenzy of greed and indulges in an orgy of envy, and these are not accidental features but the very causes of its expansionist success. The policies that are ensued through the assistance of global institutions at the pretext of lending a hand to the developing countries especially in the field of agriculture is aiming at accumulation and are not the participatory in nature. The power equations and self-governance of communities and nations are challenged through policies that ensure minimal interference. Globalisation of agriculture is largely catering to the rich nations and corporations worldwide, while traditional farming communities in the third world are choked to death and destruction by imposing hegemonic policies ensued through global institutions.

e. Economic Progress as Development: De-learning the Popular

Development has been defined in innumerable ways. However, 'Development' is generally understood to be

---

[18] E.F.Schumacher, *Small is Beautiful...*, 8.

economic growth. In this paradigm economic indictors are used to measure the growth or stagnation of economy of a country. Though economic progress is an essential component of development, it is not the only component. Nevertheless, the contention is that the 'economic achievements' as witnessed globally did not ensure an equitable growth. Schumacher contests the very terminology of being 'economic'. For him the inherent meaning of being 'economic' is when something earns an adequate profit in terms of money. Moreover, for him, economics deals with goods in accordance with their market value and not in accordance with what they really are. "The same rules and criteria are applied to primary goods, which man (sic) has to win from nature, and secondary goods, which presuppose the existence of primary goods and are manufactured from them. All goods are treated the same, because the point of view is fundamentally that of private profit-making, and this means that it is inherent in the methodology of economics to ignore man's (sic) dependence on the natural world"[19]. Increasingly, the tendency is to bring agriculture also under the gamut of economic category. This is largely assisted by trade, technological innovations, specially genetic engineering and biotechnology. The capitalistic approach to biotechnology portrays the evolution of the technology as self-determined and views social sacrifice and sacrifice of human rights including the right to livelihood as a necessity in order to give way for property rights[20]. These property rights are nevertheless not community rights rather individual rights and corporate rights. The shift from common rights to private property rights is therefore

---

[19] E.F.Schumacher, *op.cit.,* 43.

[20] The Latin root of private property, *privare,* means 'to deprive'.

a general social and political precondition for exclusivist technologies to take root in society[21]. Modernisation based on resource-hungry processes materially impoverishes communities which use those resources for survival, either directly, or through their ecological function[22]. The introduction of ecologically and economically inappropriate science and technology brings underdevelopment instead of development. [T]hat... the idea of unlimited economic growth, more and more until everybody is saturated with wealth, needs to be seriously questioned on at least two counts: the availability of basic resources and, alternatively or additionally, the capacity of the environment to cope with the degree of interference implied[23]. The economic categories aim at the quantitative, productive and trade-oriented philosophies of growth. On the other hand, a just, equitable and sustainable development paradigm that ensures qualitative, participatory, mutuality and democratic growth is envisioned to keep the present as well as the future secure.

f. Bible and Development Paradigms

In spite of being unable to provide concrete answers to 'development' pertaining to particular contexts and time frame, inferences are drawn from the Bible to evaluate development. It is generally understood that, God is the creator of the entire Universe and all the creations inhabiting it. Development as understood in its totality or wholeness includes human as well as the entire creation. Godwin Shiri has brought in the interconnectedness of

---

[21] Vandana Shiva, "Biotechnological Development and the Conservation of Biodiversity", in Vandana Shiva, Ingunn Moser, eds., *Biopolitics-A Feminist and Ecological Reader in Biotechnology* (London: Zed Books Ltd, 1995), 194.

[22] *Ibid.,* 195.

[23] E.F.Schumacher, *Small is Beautiful...,* 30.

human, nature and the Bible: "[N]ature has ... a sacred divine purpose in it. The Bible does not uphold an anthropocentric view. Human beings should have a caring, preserving and conserving attitude towards nature"[24]. The over riding emphasis in the Bible with regard to human relationship with nature is on human responsibility for nature[25]. Further, human control is needed in maintaining the cosmos over against the threat of chaos. If human breaks the covenant, then creation will return to the primeval chaos. To maintain creation, human participation is inevitable. Human participation is also needed to keep the earth fertile and productive (Genesis. 2:15, 3: 17-19). Human responsibility for the whole creation is to participate in God's continuing act of creation and recreation. Bible also speaks about the justice concerns associated to development. In Mathew 25:29, it is stated, "For unto everyone that hath shall be given and he *(sic)* shall have abundance, but from him *(sic)* that hath not, shall be taken away even that which he *(sic)* hath". Agriculture globalisation, in principle is taking away the resources that are attached to communities and caters to a minority around the world to prosper. The technological gains are profusely used to tap the resources without limits. This is violence on nature and undoubtedly will lead to imbalance in nature. Escalating calamities and global warming are examples that caution us to rethink our attitude to nature and its resources. Moreover biodiversity is essential for survival. In the Bible, Noah

---

[24] Godwin Shiri, "Ethical Perspectives of Human Development", in *Towards a Theology of Human Development*, edited by R.Gomez (Delhi: ISPCK, 1998), 162.

[25] K.C.Abraham, "Human Responsibility for the Liberation of Creation", in *Ecology and Development-Theological Perspectives*, edited by Daniel.M Chetti (Madras: UELCI/GURUKUL&BTE/SSC, 1991), 80.

had to take representatives of all species into the ark in order to make life after the flood possible[26]. The loss of species which is increasing day by day is one of the greatest dangers facing humankind. Monoculture based development agendas in the agriculture sector is a threat to the existing variety of agriculture species and diversity. This will also reinstate the hegemony of corporates over natural resources.

While human aim at temporary gains at the cost of natural resources human should not forget that it will definitely rebound at the whole creation. Human beings are entrusted to be responsible creation. There are three different ways suggested by K.C. Abraham in understanding the relations between humans and nature in the Bible[27]: 1) Humans above nature, 2) Humans in nature and 3) Humans with nature. 'Humans with nature' is assumed to be a better typology to understand the Biblical view of the relation between human and nature. Humans are part of the nature yet they are distinct from it, but this difference is not to claim superiority. According to K.C. Abraham, "[T]he Lordship...the overriding emphasis in the Bible with regard to human relationship with nature is on human responsibility for nature"[28]. All distractions of creation compounded by human violence, disobedience and greed will have to be redeemed in Christ[29]. The emphasis is that human are responsible to respond to the Biblical values of relationship between human and other creations.

---

[26] Bas Wielenga, *Towards an Eco-Just Society* (Bangalore: Centre for Social Action, 1999), 29.

[27] K.C. Abraham, *op.cit.*, 79.

[28] K.C. Abraham, *op.cit.*, 80.

[29] *Ibid.*, 81.

g. Participating Collectively with God's Creations

It is asserted that "reconciliation of man with the natural world is no longer merely desirable, it has become a necessity"[30]. God is concerned with the development and growth of the whole creation. Human beings are entrusted for the care, concern and development of the whole creation. Hence it is pertinent to know that the life-giving qualities (resources) of human beings in relationship to God is the primary focus of the Bible. There are many Biblical concepts that bring out the relatedness between human and nature and human responsibility for nature[31]. Stewardship is one such concept which is used to express the idea that the ruler of God's people is a steward, responsible to Yahweh himself (Isaiah 22: 15-21)[32]. In the New Testament Steward and Servant are used interchangeably (Mathew. 20:8); Stewards are answerable to the Master, Christ himself[33]. *Theological thinking in response to God's call has however moved a step further from the perception of welfare and stewardship to responsibility and rights issues.*

h. Development as Wholeness

Globalisation of agriculture is not a neutral process. An alliance forged by the forces of domination for profit becomes the driving force of much of globalising phenomenon in the agriculture sector. It is evident in the process of agriculture globalisation that the policies associated with it are highlighting the aspirations of a few countries, which is seeking for a world order that

---

[30] E.F. Schumacher, *Small is Beautiful...*, 114.
[31] K.C.Abraham, *Human Responsibility* ..., 81.
[32] *Ibid.*
[33] *Ibid.*

permeates the ideology of dominion, economic advancement and surplus accumulation. According to Celso Furtado, a Brazilian economist, there exist two basic forms of appropriation of surplus value since the dawn of history[34]. One is the 'authoritarian form' which consists in extracting surplus through coercion. The other is mercantile form, or acquisition of surplus though the framework of the means of trade and exchange. The authoritarian form for him appears in history when one nation or social group comes to dominate or subjugate another[35]. But the mercantile form is found not simply in the processes of trade, but particularly related to a process of expanding productivity, which ultimately come to take possession of the surplus[36].

The *Pastoral Constitution on the Church in the Modern World* of the Second Vatican Council describes the present fragileness of 'development'[37]:

> "Never has the human race enjoyed such an abundance of wealth, resources and economic power. Yet a huge proportion of the world's citizen is still tormented by hunger and poverty, while countless number suffers from total illiteracy. Never before today has man (sic) been so keenly aware of freedom, yet at the same time, new forms of social and psychological slavery make their appearance".

The 'development' initiated through the process of globalising the agriculture sector caters to a minority and their insatiability. Nevertheless, development in its

---

[34] Leornado Boff and Virgil Elizondo, *Option for the Poor: Challenge to the Rich Countries* (Edinburgh: T&T Clark Ltd, 1986), 12.

[35] Leornado Boff and Virgil Elizondo, *Option for the Poor...*, 5.

[36] *Ibid.*, 6.

[37] *The Church Today*, No.4, cited by Peter Remigius, *Towards a Theology of Development* (Delhi: ISPCK, 1998), 4.

authentic and Biblical sense should cater to all equally and sustainably.

One of the underlying principles of globalisation is economic advancement and the main subject matter of economics is 'goods'. Schumacher challenges this reductionism of development which has its foundations purely on economic categories. For him, while economists categorise goods into consumer and producer goods, what is ignored is to define what such goods actually are; whether they are man-made or God-given , whether they are freely reproducible or not. Any goods that are appeared on the market are treated as the same, as objects for sale and nothing more. But Schumacher's contention is that, secondary products are dependent on primary products from the earth and man (sic) is not a producer rather a converter of primary goods to which we are dependent on nature[38]. Hence nature has to be treated cautiously in order to maintain the renewability of resources. Globalisation of agriculture proposes monoculture based production which is derogatory to the renewability of resources. Attempts to reap benefits on an immediate and quantitative scale will lead to the destruction of primary resources. Thus the concept of 'development' should transcend its mere 'economic' category and necessitates a more inclusive and wholesome approach. We are committed to a vision of human wholeness which includes our relationship with nature and the universe not just because we are dependent on nature for our survival, rather a God-given responsibility to be in harmony with all of God's creation.

---

[38] E.F.Schumacher, *Small is Beautiful...*, 50.

i. Sustainability of Nature as well as Human Existence

To ensure sustainable development without damaging the natural resources base, the basic life support systems-soil, water, flora and fauna, and the environment are to be nurtured and protected for enhancing agricultural production. The Brundtland Commission Report describes sustainable development as follows: "Sustainable development meets the needs of the present without compromising the ability of future generations to meet their own needs"[39]. The interconnectedness between commitment of the renewal of society and the renewal of earth is necessary in maintaining sustainability. Development projects, especially globalisation of agriculture inevitably involve a major shift in the way rights to resources are perceived. Privatisation of resources ensued through globalisation deprives weaker sections their right to survival and will also prevents the nature its right to self-renewal. This will turn around the balance in mutuality between human and nature.

j. Towards Evolving a Mutual Subsistence Paradigm

A key value central to sustainable development is that of responsibility. 'Responsibility' reminds us of the responsibility entrusted in us to play our role and the impact it reciprocates. This also reminds us of the interconnectedness between human and non-human living species. The justice concerns the right relationships between human beings and human and other segments of creation. Sustainable agriculture is based on the recycling of soil nutrients. This involves returning to the soil, part of the nutrients that come from the soil either directly as organic fertiliser, or indirectly through the manure from farm

---

[39] *www.earthcharter.com.*

animals. Maintenance of the nutrient cycle, and through it the fertility of the soil, is based on this inviolable law of return, which is a timeless, essential element of sustainable agriculture[40]. Hence diversity needs to be affirmed and agriculture practices that enhances sustainability needs to be promoted instead of productivity and trade being elevated to the status of being inevitable necessities to growth.

Conclusion

Globalisation of agriculture extends beyond communities and nations. Several pertinent queries emerge in connection with this seemingly 'unavoidable' development paradigm of globalisation. Did globalisation of agriculture achieve a justifiable and equitable growth? Does better productivity envisioned through technological innovations achieve the targeted results and brought down disparities? Who are the beneficiaries of this process? What are the impacts of technological innovations upon agriculture, nature and its existence? The analysis done is a pointer to the ideology enshrined in agriculture globalisation that has negative impacts on human and non-human life. The undergirding development paradigm of agriculture globalisation is contested from various levels. Based on a sustainable model of development paradigm, it is understood that human needs, self-reliance and organic articulation are the foundations on which human development should be constructed. The focus is on diversity and autonomy of spaces. However, the right over natural resources like land, water and seeds are largely being concentrated in the process initiated through the globalisation of

---

[40] Vandana Shiva, *Monocultures of the Mind* (Dehradun: Natraj Publishers, 1993), 57.

agriculture. This hegemony is questioned and democratisation, participation, and rights are asserted in the sustainable process in which solutions to specific needs and problems are dealt from the bottom upwards. The primary question is not of trade and profit rather of human needs in a viable and self-reliant environment. The ethical question will also be, how much further 'growth' will be possible since unlimited growth in a limited environment is an obvious impossibility. The technological pursuit that enthralls India today is hardly the "appropriate" or "intermediate" technology urged by E.F. Schumacher's Small is Beautiful (1973)[41]. Rather it strives to be large and succeeds in being ugly. Its energy intensive applications and its fossil fuel dependency are hardly sustainable as we reach the ecological limits of the carrying capacity of our increasingly fragile environment[42]. The introduction of ecologically and economically inappropriate science and technology is leading to underdevelopment instead of development. The neglect of the role of natural resources in ecological processes and in people's sustenance economy, and the diversion and destruction of these resources for commodity production and capital accumulation are the main reasons for the agricultural crisis. The solution seems to lie in giving local communities control over local resources so that they have the right and responsibility to rebuild nature's economy, and through it, their sustenance. Furthermore, globalisation of agriculture prescribes universal external knowledge systems suitable elsewhere, while context specific knowledge systems are neglected in

---

[41] Rudolf C Heredia, "Inclusive Development, Liberating Modernity: India Civilization at the Crossroads.1", Vidyajyoti Journal of Theological Reflection, Vol.71, Jan-Dec. 2007, 37.

[42] Ibid.

order to assert control. A shift from the globalising to the local knowledge is important because it frees knowledge from the dependency on established regimes of thought, making it more autonomous and more authentic.

It is evident in the analysis that globalisation of agriculture did not cater to the whole humanity evenly; rather it has increased the disparities. Furthermore, the target of feeding the poor remains a myth. Power relations are ever widening and concentration of power is ever increasing. The beneficiaries are the powerful and the rich capitalistic nations. The touchstone of capitalist economics is the maximisation of profit, ie, the accumulation of capital (property), which is measured in money. The achievement of this fundamental aim depends on the success of competition with other capital owners in the production and marketing of goods[43]. Plant-based bio-technology, genetic engineering and genetically modified seeds and other scientific revolutions that occur in agricultural bio-technology have created new avenues and space for agri-business TNC's to maximise profits. In the current globalising era, the IMF-WB-TNC's-WTO and G-7, the so-called economically powerful groups, are the advocates of liberalising markets and thus benefit from the outcome of reforms with their market power[44]. The traditional belief systems of sustenance, mutuality and need based economy that catered to humanity in the past has given way to trade, monocultures, and hegemonic control over resources which are beneficial to a minority

---

[43] Ulrich Duchrow & Franz J Hinkelammert, *Property for People, not for Profit: Alternatives to the Global Tyranny of Capital*, (Geneva: WCC Publications, 2004), 91.

[44] I. John Mohan Razu, "Food, A Human Right: An Ethical Perspective", in John Mohan Razu (ed.), *Struggle for Human Rights* (Nagpur: National Council of Churches in India, 2001), 35-68.

to prosper inexhaustibly. Biblical paradigms reassert the ethical principle of responsibility of the whole creation. Humans are invited to be in harmony with co-creatures to creatively participate in the creation. Principles of dominion, exploitation, coercion and unevenness are condemned in the Biblical witness to liberate creation. Freedom is an asserted ethical principle in the Bible which accentuates freedom from all sorts of bondages. Hegemony reinstated through dominating the under-developed as well as the non-human creatures is thus contradictory to Biblical ethical principles. This dominion challenges the mutuality as well as the question of sustenance. In spite of being contributive in certain ways to humanity, the basic principles that guide globalisation of agriculture is largely impacting the majority negatively.

BIBLIOGRAPHY

Agarwal, B.L., ed. *Alternative Economic Structures*. New Delhi: Indian Institute of Advanced Studies and Allied Publishers, 1989.

Alagh, Yoginder. *The Great Grain Drain*. Bangalore: Books for Change, 1998.

Bisht, Singh Devendra. *Agriculture Development in India*. New Delhi: Anmol Publications, 1989.

Boff, Leornado and Virgil Elizondo, eds. *Option for the Poor. Challenge to the Rich Countries*. Edinburgh: T&T Clark Ltd, 1986.

Chetti, D. Daniel., ed. *Ecology and Development*. Madras: UELCI/GURUKUL & BTE/ SSC, 1991.

Dogra, Bharat. *Seeds Industry of India: Seeds of Plenty or Seeds of Discontent*. New Delhi: Navdanya and NFS-India, 1993.

Duchrow, Ulrich and Franz J Hinkelammert. *Property for People, Not for Profit. Alternatives to the Global Tyranny of Capital*. Geneva: WCC Publications, 2004.

Elliott, Charles. *The Development Debate*. London: SCM Press, 1971.

Gadgil, Madhav, et al., *Ecology and Equity*. New Delhi: Penguin Books, 1995.

George, Susan. *A Fate Worse Than Debt*. New York: Grove Weidenfeld, 1990.

Gomez, R, ed. *Towards a Theology of Development*. Delhi: ISPCK, 1998.

Heimstra, Wim., Coen Reijntjes and Erik Van Der Weif, eds. *Let Farmers Judge. Experiences in Assessing the Sustainability of Agriculture.* London: Intermediate Technology Publications, 1992.

Jodha, N.S. *Sustainable Development in Fragile Environments.* Ahmedabad: Centre for Environment Education, 1995.

Johnson, A.A. *Indian Agriculture in the 1970's.* New Delhi: Ford Foundation, 1970.

Joshi, B.K., ed. *Alternative Development Strategies and the Indian Experience.* Bombay: Himalaya Publishing House, 1984.

Khor, Martin. *Rethinking Globalisation.* Bangalore: Books for Change, 2001.

Kothari, Ashish. *Understanding Biodiversity.* New Delhi: Orient Longman, 1997.

Kumar, Krishna, ed. *GATT, WTO and Indian Agriculture.* Delhi: Farm Digest Publications, 1996.

Madeley, John. *Food for All. Can Hunger be Halved?.* London: The Panos Institute, 2001.

Madhav, Gadgil, et al., *Ecology and Equity: The Use and Abuse of Nature in Contemporary India.* New Delhi: Penguin Books, 1995.

McDonagh, Sean. *Passion for the Earth.* Maryknoll: Orbis Books, 1994.

Muricken, Ajith, ed. *Globalisation and SAP Trends and Impact-An Overview.* Mumbai: Vikas Adhyayan Kendra, 1997.

Perriere, De La, Robert Ali Brac and Franck Seuret. *Brave New Seeds: The Threat of GM Crops To Farmers.* London: Zed Books, 2000.

Peter Remigius. *Towards a Theology of Development* Delhi: ISPCK, 1998.

Raj, K.N. *Organizational Issues in Indian Agriculture.* Delhi: Oxford University Press, 1990.

Reijntjes, Coen. *Farming for the Future: An Introduction to Low-External Input and Sustainable Agriculture.* London: Macmillan Press, 1992.

Robinson, Gnana. *Challenges and Responses-Church's Ministry in the Third Millennium. Implications for Theological Education.* Bangalore: Asian Trading Corporation, 2000.

Roy, Sumit. *Globalisation, ICT and Developing Nations.* New Delhi: Sage Publications, 2005.

Rudra, Ashok. *Political Economy of Indian Agriculture.* Calcutta: K P Bagchi and Co., 1992.

Sheth, Pravin. *Environmentalism: Politics, Ecology and Development.* Jaipur: Rawat Publications, 1997.

Schumacher, E.F. *Small Is Beautiful: Economics as if People Mattered.* New York: Harper & Row Publishers, 1975.

Shiva, Vandana. *Betting On Biodiversity.* New Delhi: Research Foundation for Science, Technology and Ecology, 2006.

Shiva, Vandana and Ingunn Moser, eds. *Biopolitics: A Feminist and Ecological Reader in Biotechnology.* London: Zed Books, 1995.

Shiva, Vandana, et al., *Corporate Hijack of Agriculture.* New Delhi: Navdanya, 2002.

_____. *Genetic Modification and Frankenstein Foods: The Ecological Risks of Genetic Engineering in Agriculture.* New Delhi: Navdanya, 2000.

_____. *Globalisation of Agriculture.* New Delhi: Research Foundation for Science, Technology and Ecology, 2000.

_____. *Globalisation of Agriculture and the Growth of Food Insecurity.* New Delhi: Research Foundation for Science, Technology and Natural Resource Policy, 1996.

Shiva, Vandana. *Globalisation of Agriculture Food Security and Sustainability.* New Delhi: Research Foundation for Science, Technology and Ecology, 1999.

_____., et al., *How Globalisation is Destroying Farmers and Livelihoods.* New Delhi: Navdanya Research Foundation for Science, Technology and Ecology, 2003.

_____. *Monocultures of the Mind.* DehraDun: Natraj Publishers, 1993.

_____., et al., *The Mirage Of Market Access.* New Delhi: Navdanya Research Foundation for Science, Technology and Ecology, 2003.

_____. *Violence of the Green Revolution. Third World Agriculture: Ecology and Politics.* Mapusa: Other India Press. 1992.

Veeresh, G.K., ed. *Organic Farming for Alleviation of Rural Poverty.* Bangalore: Association for Promotion of Organic Farming, 2006.

Wielenga, Bas. *Towards an Eco-Just Society.* Bangalore: Centre for Social Action, 1999.

Articles in Books

Abraham, K.C. "Human Responsibility for the Liberation of Creation." In *Ecology and Development- Theological Perspectives.* Daniel. M. Chetti., ed. Madras: UELCI/ GURUKUL & BTE/SSC, 1991.

Aziz, Abdul. "Manifestation of Globalisation." In *Globalisation-Marginalization of Women, Dalits and Tribals.* Viswanath Rosemanry, ed. Bangalore: Solidarity, 1998.

Hobbelink, Henk. "Biotechnology and the Future of Agriculture." In *Biopolitics: A Feminist and Ecological Reader on Biotechnology.* Vandana Shiva and Ingunn Moser eds. London: Zed Books Ltd, 1995.

Perlas, Nicanor. "The Seven Dimensions of Sustainable Agriculture." In *Biopolitics: A Feminist and Ecological Reader on Biotechnology*. Vandana Shiva and Ingunn Moser eds. London: Zed Books Ltd, 1995.

Razu, I. John Mohan. "Food, A Human Right: An Ethical Perspective." In *Struggle for Human Rights*. John Mohan Razu ed. Nagpur: National Council of Churches in India, 2001.

Shiri, Godwin. "Ethical Perspectives of Human Development." In *Towards a Theology of Human Development*. R.Gomez., ed. Delhi: ISPCK, 1998.

Shiva, Vandana. "Biotechnological Development and the Conservation of Biodiversity." In *Biopolitics-A Feminist and Ecological Reader in Biotechnology*. Vandana Shiva and Ingunn Moser, eds. London: Zed Books Ltd, 1995.

——————. "The Green Revolution and After." In *The Great Grain Drain*. Bangalore: Books for Change, 1998.

——————. "Democracy in the Age of Globalisation." In *Globalisation and SAP: Trends &Impact- An Overview*. Ajit Muricken, ed. Mumbai: Vikas Adhyayan Kendra, 1997.

Patil, S.A. and H.B.Babalad. "Organic Farming and Sustainable Agriculture-Key Issues." In *Organic Inputs for Organic Farming*. G.K. Veeresh, ed., Bangalore: Association for Promotion of Organic Farming, 2002.

Articles in Journals

Anne McGuirk, "The Doha Development Agenda." *Finance and Development* 39/3 (September, 2002): 3-9

Banerjee, Brojendra Nath. "Globalisation of Agriculture." *Religion and Society*, XLI/ 2 (June, 1994): 46-61.

Berg Andrew and Anne Krueger, "Lifting All Boats." *Finance and Development* 39/3 (September, 2002): 15-18.

"Editorial Column." *People's Reporter*, 19/13 (July 10-25, 2006):2

"Editorial Column." *People's Reporter*, 20/2 (January 25-February 10, 2007): 2

Hans, Peter Lankes, "Market Access for Developing Countries." *Finance and Development* 39/3 (September, 2002): 10-13.

Heredia, Rudolf C. "Inclusive Development, Liberating Modernity: Indic Civilization at the Crossroads.1." *Vidyajyoti Journal of Theological Reflection* 71/1 (December-January, 2007): 28-42.

Koshy, Ninan. "The Global Empire."*Peoples' Reporter* 19/15 (August: 10-25, 2006):3-7.

Pradit Takerngrangsarit, "The God That Bush Worships Is Not Our God." *People's Reporter* 19/20 (October 25-November 10, 2006): 3-5.

"Protect the Farmers and Cancel the Debts." *People's Reporter* 20/3 (February 10-25, 2007): 1-4.

Ragahavan, V.P. "Agricultural Trade Policy and Food Security in India: Issues and Challenges." *Social Action* 56/1 (January-March):1-10

Razu, I. John Mohan. "Ideology of Life and Theology of Resistance: A Framework for the Present." *Bangalore Theological Forum* 33/2 (December, 2001): 140-153.

Sustainable Agriculture is More Profitable." *Frontline* 22/15, (Jul 16-29, 2005): 12-16.

Weil, Robert. "Doomed Harvest." *Multinational Monitor* 21/5 (May, 2000): 16-18.

Entries in Encyclopedia

"Genetic Engineering." *Microsoft® Encarta® 99 Encyclopedia.* © 1993-1998 Microsoft Corporation.

Reports and Papers

Organization for Economic Co-operation, Development and Environmental Benefit from Agriculture: Issues and Policies. The Helsinki Seminar. New Delhi: Oxford and IBH Publishing Co., 1998.

"The People vs Global Capital: The G-7, TNC's, SAP's and Human Rights." *Report of the International People's Tribunal to Judge the G-7. Tokyo, July 1993*, Japan: PARC, 1994.

S, Ambirajan. Papers. United Theological College. (Bangalore) 29 July1998.

World Development Report 2003. *Sustainable Development in a Dynamic World Transforming Institutions, Growth and Quality of Life.* New York: Oxford University Press, 2003.

Newspapers

Deccan Herald, 27 April 2001.

Deccan Herald, 16 June 2001.

Deccan Herald, 2 August 2002.

Deccan Herald, 2 September 2003.

Deshabhimani, 23 November, 2006.

Deshabhimani Daily, 29 November 2006.

Malayala Manorama, 1 February 2007.

The Hindu, 18 March 2003.

Electronic Sources

Editorial, *"Nelvayalukal Samrakshikkanam".* *www.deshabhimani.com/news/k5.htm,* (14 July 2006).

JohnElkerd."Globalisation."*http://www.ssu.missouri.edu/Faculty/JIkerd/papers/Globalisation.html* (25 Oct 2006).

Mittal, Anuradha. "Land Loss, Poverty and Hunger." *International Forum on Globalisation,* (3 December 2001): *http:// www. alternet.org/globalisation/*12001/ (7 Feb 2007).

Sharma, Devinder. "Food Supremacy: America's Other War," 13 February, 2002 *www.fpif.org/outside/commentary/2002/0202food_body.html.* (24 November 2006).

Shiva,Vandana. "The Indian Seed Act and Patent Act: Sowing the Seeds of Dictatorship." *http//: www. zmag.org/content/showarticle.cfm?ItemID=7249* (31 January 2007).

"The challenge of global environment: Education for a sustainable future." *http//: www.sgi.org/do/ngo-resources/proposal.html.* (1 December 2006)

Victoria, Tauli- Corpuz. "Biotechnology and Indigenous People Source." *http://www. wcc-coe.org/wcc/what/jpc/trips2.html-9k* (12 November 2006).

"Biodiversity and Genetic Resources." *www.etcgroup.org/en/issues/biodiversity_genetic_resources.html* (12 November 2006).